Books by the same author

Oops! 'I' fell in Love!

Ouch! that 'Hearts'..

SHE IS SINGLE
I'M TAKEN
AND WE'RE COMMITTED...

Harsh Snehanshu

Srishti
PUBLISHERS & DISTRIBUTORS

Srishti Publishers & Distributors
N-16, C. R. Park
New Delhi 110 019
srishtipublishers@gmail.com

First published by
Srishti Publishers & Distributors in 2012

Copyright © Harsh Snehanshu 2012
2nd impression,
All characters in this book are fictitious, and any resemblance to real persons, living or dead, is coincidental.

Typeset by EGP at Srishti

Printed and bound in India

All rights reserved. No part of this publication may be reproduced, stored in a retrieval system, or transmitted, in any form or by any means, electronic, mechanical, photocopying, recording or otherwise, without the prior written permission of the Publishers.

*This book is dedicated to my favorite reader,
Late Ms. Anuranjani Verma, 1990-2012
I'm sorry, for not being able to
finish this book on time.
Wish you could hold it in your hand.*

ACKNOWLEDGEMENTS

It's always very difficult to write a sequel to a book. And writing a sequel to a sequel is something that every first time writer would dread. Before I begin this book, let me tell you that I'm afraid. Afraid whether I'll be able to maintain the flow that I managed to maintain in the earlier two books, whether I'll be doing justice to the characters that I created, whether this part is necessary or not and so on. But at the back of my mind, I realize that every story, much like every character, has a destiny and it's not fulfilled if it is left unfinished. It is my duty as an author to complete Kanav-Tanya's tale and give the reader the delight of knowing a complete story.

I thank my readers for their enormous love. They made my debut characters stay in my life for such a long period. I feel sad at their prospective departure from my life after the end of this book and I could just pray that their erroneous love story remains imprinted in your memory for life to come.

I acknowledge Saumya Snehil for designing the ambigram that's there in this book. Yes, even this book has an ambigram! This acknowledgment would not be complete if I don't thank my school friend and a very talented writer: Anant Utkarsh, for going through the manuscript critically and offering me keen insights to improve it.

I would like to specifically thank some of my friends and readers who have kept me motivated all the while: Tripti Goel, Prerana Vyas,

Tusharika Deka, Ramita Manocha, Sharmistha Mitra, Raheela Baksh, Priya Vatsalam, Gargi Trehan, Geetika Khanna, Abhijit Sarmah, Shivam Jindal, Amit Anand(golu), Juhi Mahadik, Anirudh Hothur, Soumya Mukherjee, Arjun Bhatia, Nitisha Pandey, Shubham Chaudhary, Vajpayeeji(once again!), Naval Dhunna(novey dovey), Chitra Signodiya, Jayati Agarwal, Ankita Mohanta, Tanya Gupta, Swity Singh, Isha Monga, Tushant Baranwal, Aarti Mathur, Nidhi Kaushik, Mohit Gupta, Sandipan Biswas, Swarna Agarwalla, Varun Yadav, Henna Multani(Eos), Saket Jajodia, Sourabh Goyal, Ashish Jhanwar, Tushant Barnwal, Nikhil Mukhija, Madhusudan Singh Tomar(hippie), Nithya Mouli, Richa Joshi, Guramanbir Singh, Charu Smita, Umakant Vashishtha, Mridul Kanti Roy Chowdhary(MKRC), Rirshi Bhargava, Kanul Sharma, Deepanshu Nihalani, Shivang Chopra, Siddharth Awadhoot, Dhruv Jain, Prerana Vatsa, Rajeev Mahadevan, Aman Hooda – my first reader, and many more.

I had promised my readers connected to me on facebook that I would give them an opportunity to gift their special one something really special. Here it is. I heartily acknowledge some very special people, who have been an unforgettable part of some of my readers' lives: Archit Goyal, Vedika Marodia, Chetan Barak, Akanksha Bindal, Mayank Saxena, Chirag Chamoli, Palaash Pradhanani, Haramit Dhillon, Sheela Shinde, Elwin, Ankita Roy Choudhury, Hemina Baldota, Nishita Serrao, Jake, Mansi Jain, Shradhha Chauhan, Alekhya Paladugula, Ansari Kashish Jamal, Prashant Mantri, Abhishek Sarkar, Vinayak Mishra, Kuldeep Joshi, Yashraj Dighe, Neha Singh, Nishi, Abhilash, Navjot Bhatia, Rishab Mehtani, Rohit Mantri, Prashant Rajput, Rohit Mantri, Sumit Biswas, Surabhi Jha, Kirti Jangra, Shubhankar Sharma, Aman Agha, Asish Sarma Thakur, Sanka, Popat, Megha and Gaurav.

For the cover design of this novel, I had conducted a contest. I was very touched by the response that I got in the contest. Though I could shortlist just one winner, I take this opportunity to acknowledge all the contributors here: Shikha Mishra, Ketan Maniya, Kirtan Joshi, Angshuk Ghosh, Deepti Pareek, Kashish Vaidya, Rabijit Dey, Manipal Singh, Saumya Chawdhary, Manali Parmar, Gaurav Jha, Ila Singh, Sachin Shresta, Bhaskar Waji, Manali Joshi, Hitanshi Rawal, Akanksha Shrivastava and Aparajita Shrivastava. Special thanks to the talented designers Shikha Mishra, Ketan Maniya and Kirtan Joshi for patiently undertaking iterations, before the finalization of the cover.

Also, I would like to thank my friends and authors Sachin Garg and Sudeep Nagarkar for helping me at every moment, whenever I faced any doubts related to writing or publishing.

Hope this part fulfills the destiny of Kanav and Tanya.

'Love's not love, until love's vulnerable.'

                                        - Theodore Roethke

From Ouch! That 'hearts'..

12th February, 2008

It's not about you or me or us. It's not about the fact that we dated or we had been in love. It's about respect. In the last 24 hours, no matter how hard I tried to convince myself, your harsh words echoed in my ears and made me tremble every single time. I feel emotionally raped. You've been consistently saying that it was a silly reason why I got frenzied, but as a woman, and as a lover, I feel shattered. Disrespect is worse than betrayal, Kanav. It breaks the very essence of a relationship.

Maybe you didn't mean what you said; maybe you wanted to say something else and accidentally showed the dark side of yours. But what if you meant everything you said, when you said that I was no more than an average loser stuck in your life from nowhere, when you said that I was the biggest mistake of your life, when you dared to not only abuse me but went on to my mother. You couldn't have said that if you didn't mean it, no matter how angry you would have been. It hurts, Kanav. It hurts a lot. I've never felt this bad, since there always had been the faith that somebody loved me more than I ever desired, that kept me going but last day, you even took that faith away from me and now I'm nothing more than a woman wasted in love.

I couldn't believe my ears when I heard you last time. I thought it couldn't be you. It couldn't be my Kanav. I thought so because I cared. But, you didn't. You went on; until you made sure that you shredded every bit of love from within me. Maybe I don't mean anything to you. Or maybe I do. I don't know. And the truth is, I don't want to know anymore. I've lost everything I had. I always wished my love to be utopian, uncontaminated with any such ill events. But this has taken away my power even to wish. How could I ever be convinced that you didn't mean what you said? Your words won't convince me, since your words can't stand strong against your own words.

You need to fight with yourself first. I don't think it's the right time for us to be together because where there's lack of respect; there'll be lack of love. I'll be gone in a day and I would give you ample space to introspect, come face to face with yourself, realize whether it is love or anything else that is holding you on to me, for love is built on respect. Learn to respect. And before that, respect respect.

I'll not wait for you. I might move on with my life and would love if you do the same. I'll be happy. I have all the more reasons to be happy since now I'll no more be guilty of lying to my mother. Kanav, it's my humble request to you that if you actually love me, please do not ever try to reach me. Let's stand this test of sacrifice; if we're destined to be together, nothing could stop us.

I loved you. Take care.

Tanya

Chapter 1:
INTRODUCTION

13th February, 2008

Every time I say I won't remember you, I end up remembering you. This time I would stick to my words. I'm a man of words: I should live up to my image. When you were there, I could very easily deny the fact that I love you, sometimes just to play around with you, sometimes just to hurt you. But now when you are gone, I can't deny it. Not even once. I love you. More than I ever realized I could. You, your perpetual happiness, your smile when you were standing on the other side of the road, your peculiar laugh, your brisk walk, your slender fingers, your captivating smell, your silky hair, your little-bit-hairy neck, your perfect toes, your small feet, your glistening white teeth and those big gums - the only imperfection in you that made you a little bit imperfect - thus perfect for me - cloud my mind all the time. In the last twenty four hours, there hasn't been a moment when I didn't think about you. I can't understand why thinking about you always makes me cry. I'm a strong mar, I have always told myself. Now when you're gone, I realize that you were my strength. I wish I could have been the person who could keep you happy. I wish I could touch your heart again as I did once upon a time. I wish you had never gone. I wish you were here. I wish you loved me. I wish all my wishes come true. You come true. We come true.

I wish. I wish many things. Some realistic, some not. And some, just needful.

As I begin to complete my love story I have many thoughts in my mind. Whether this story would end. What does it mean when I say an end? Does it need an end?

Day by day, if you observe me right from my first book, I've changed – as a person, as an individual, as a lover, as a human being. Changed for good or bad, I do not know. I've changed so much that I think it is the right time to reintroduce myself here.

Hello, I'm Kanav Bajaj. The name still sounds cool, isn't it? I have a strange habit. I'm always concerned about what others are thinking about me. That makes me self-deprecating at times and sarcastic at other times, just to look intellectual. If I am placed in front of an honest mirror, it would reflect that I'm a moron, a self-obsessed jerk and a person mad in love. *Yes.*

She has left me, this time by her own choice – a choice which I respect, a choice which I understand and a choice that has drawn me closer to her. I don't expect her to come back. I do wish, however. I wish a lot. I wish that some things didn't happen. I wish I hadn't said some things. I wish I was not in love. I wish my life were as dreamlike as it was on the first day. I wish she wasn't there. I wish … oh why do I wish?

Remorse. It's the worst feeling in this world. It exhausts you, it sucks your blood, it makes you despise yourself and it makes you what you are not. This story begins where it was paused the last time, the time when she consciously decided to move out of my life.

Noon
13th February, 2009

A blank sheet of MS word lay in front of my eyes. She was gone and the long awaited sequel to my first book had ended on a sad note. The blankness of the sheet didn't comfort me. I urged myself to pen down.

She has left me. But still, she is left in me.

These were the only words that I could write. The blank sheet was much better than the words that it contained now. At least it didn't make me cry earlier.

Evening
13th February, 2009

I was holding the first few copies of my book in my hand. I had decided to launch it in my hostel, in front of my friends. I hadn't told them about the disaster that happened the day before. Company of friends is always found to be better than aloofness, when remorse clouds one's mind.

Almost my entire hostel had assembled in the conference room in the basement. Sameer brought five gift-wrapped copies of my book and handed over to me. He was very eager to address the audience and I gave him the much desired opportunity. I was expecting to hear a verbose speech, full of philosophical quotes and anecdotes, but surprisingly it was an altogether different story.

Guys, it brings me immense pleasure to host this gathering, where our dear friend, Kanav has made us proud. This moment is a special moment for us, for he made our hostel – Zanskar famous in his book, and also, he'd specially acknowledged each one of us who had been encouraging in his endeavour. It is difficult to restrain my laughter, but I'm glad to inform you that he has published the fact that Aryan had been gay, Anuj had been double dating and I have been his most awesome friend out there. *wink*

Sameer's scandalous revelations incited a few furrowed eyebrows at me, who were concerned whether their personal stories made it into the book or not and if they did, had they been depicted in a slanderous manner or hilarious. Sarthak, one of my batchmates, stealthily came forward and snatched one of the gift-wrapped books from the table and ran across the basement towards the TV room. Sameer, with his heavy torso, chased him and ultimately conquered him by catching his leg. Soon, the entire inauguration event turned topsy-turvy, when two *matkes* (mtechs) decided that the best way to celebrate the launch was to get my butt roasted. I should have run then but what happened thereafter didn't allow me to write anything for the next 24 hours.

I was asked to read my favorite paragraph from my book. Assaulted, I took it as my only chance to exercise my vengeance. I read aloud an impromptu speech:

Here goes my favorite part of my book.

IIT Delhi exposed me to a strange breed of people. Almost everybody was interested in mocking one or another. Thanks to my friend Sameer, I could feel good since he was the subject of everyone's mockery almost all the time, courtesy his pumpkin-like body and irritating voice. No wonder my friends, Anuj and Aryan, who were scoundrels of greater orders, loved mocking Sameer. The rest of the hostel, including Sarthak, Manas (the one with a cigarette always stuck on his lips), Raheja and around six to seven Guptas were no more than irritating geeks, who seemed to have come straight from their schools with moustaches like uncles and interests like aunties. The rarest of the rare being the matkes, who seemed out of the place, since they didn't look like uncles, rather like grandfathers. It seemed that IIT had a special quota for appointing aging education enthusiasts. Some of them were so old that they used to get marriage proposals from retiring ladies and grannies, for their aging daughters of course.

I expected a look of shock on their face. Claps clasped my heart, followed by pleasant smiles all around. They were laughing, their eyes looking as if they had been thoroughly entertained by what I recited. I smiled back and said, 'It is not in the book.'

'Oh! Why didn't you put that? It was good.'

'I came up with that just now, will put that in the next book, what say?' I assured.

'Never before had we enjoyed our mockery so much,' one of the *matkes* mumbled in delight. He was the first buyer of my book. Soon, followed the rest of the hostel; most of them, being penniless retards, tried to persuade my agent Sameer to give them the book on credit. Sameer was ruthless. He extracted money from all of their pockets and decided that he'll keep twenty rupees per book as his royalty. Ironically, that was more than the royalty I was to get per book.

The book had a strange result on my life. The very first mail from my reader mesmerized me. It was an army person, Aman from Delhi, who related how much he had liked my book. I never thought that my writing could move someone living several miles away from me. It was enchanting. I was no more just another guy; at least people made me feel so. I was a mini-celeb, having a following of my own, with wonderful readers proclaiming statements like, 'I'm your biggest fan', 'Oops! I fell in love with you!' and sometimes even, 'Dude, let me know when you and Tanya break-up, I'm mad about her.'

In the campus, however, I experienced a strange kind of alienation. Other than my close friends, half of the crowd treated me as though I was some sinner, who had written about their dirty secrets and revealed those to the world. Unknown people used to turn hostile towards me, which I used to find very amusing, until a senior enlightened me that it was a typical IITian behaviour. They are so competitive that they can't see anyone excelling in a difficult field. They are more concerned about the fact that my book was selling than what stuff I'd written.

The first month that went once the book got published was refreshing for me. I was totally new to attention and I thoroughly loved it. I used to add every person who wrote to me in my chat-list and used to chat with them. I found some really good friends in the process, but every good thing comes at a price – a price that could even have challenged my chastity. Okay, not chastity but at least virginity. Meet the Queen of Venice.

Chapter 2:
THE QUEEN OF VENICE

It had been two months since my novel was published. The response had been stunning, much more than what I had expected. Every day over a dozen mails from readers all around India would be occupying my inbox. Some contained heart-warming praises, some contained genuine criticisms, which were in good spirit to help me improve as an author. Some were cynical, which I read and hardly cared to reply.

The sudden spurt of fame seemed wonderful, being one of the rarest feelings I've ever encountered. I was at my life's most enchanting period - the period of utmost creative joy. It was during that time that this girl with the name 'queenofvenice' read my entire work and decided to throw some brickbats in the comments section of the promotional blog for my novel. But unlike others, she had a different take on it - completely different.

'Your work was like-able but I hated you totally. If there was the word slut for a man, you would be that. I wonder how people could give you so much attention,' she wrote.

I was thoroughly entertained and a little bit confused. I liked being called a 'man-slut'. It was the rarest of compliments that one could have ever received in life. Not that I loved it for the very feel of it but it actually gave me a better opinion of myself, as far as women were concerned. That was so because my experience in this field was painfully limited.

Did she confuse me with any of the characters, or has my presence as a writer been so insipid? I showed it to Anuj, who got outraged and started typing rubbish, when I stopped and asked him to let me reply.

I began, 'Thank you. It was a pleasure getting attention from you. I didn't know that I could ever be complimented for such a cause. Thanks again.'

Within an hour, she posted another comment, 'I was not giving you attention! I was just letting you know what your status is.'

'I can't understand the reason behind your hatred. If it's my novel that's the reason, let me remind you that everything there is fictitious,' I immediately replied.

'And I would not like being called a slut in public, so shoot each of your anger-shots at me at the given id – kanav.bajaj@gmail.com,' I turned flirtatious. Her audacity being the reason for my audacity.

A moment later, *queenofvenice@gmail.com* sent me an add request. As always, carrying on with my earlier wimpish self when it came to strangers, I couldn't dare to start the chat. She took the initiative.

queenofvenice: *It's 2 o' clock at night. I'm not too fond of talking to guys at night, and more so your kind – tch tch.*

I: *Neither am I. I never talk to guys, especially at this time.*

'Thank God, for giving me a sense of humour,' I thought.

queenofvenice: *You asshole! What do you think you are?*

I felt insulted. I wanted to block her then and forever. But I was new to attention and I liked it. However, my self-respect asked my timid self to rebel. I could not tolerate the bullshit.

I: Wait a minute. Who the fuck are you?

I was suspicious that this would be a gag that one of my hostel-friends would be playing with me, at the middle of the night.

queenofvenice: *I'm a hardcore feminist. And I'm against every person who considers woman as a sex-object.*

The doubt that the Queen of Venice might be residing in my hostel almost faded. My worldly hostel-friends would never have tried to act as feminists in their entire life, not even for the sake of a gag, leave alone being a hardcore one. I tried to search her id on social networking websites, and ultimately I could find her on Facebook. Her name was Shambhavi and she seemed to be pretty. Another reason to talk. I read the conversation once again.

I: Wait a minute. Where have I talked about women as sex-objects in my novel?

queenofvenice: *You have not but your feelings were visible all throughout your piece of shit.*

I (sarcastically): Oh really, then what made you lick that piece of shit in its entirety?

queenofvenice: *You wrote it well. Engrossing, but full of shit.*

I: So, you like shit?

queenofvenice: *I hate asses, like you!*

Curious!

I: Who are you? I mean where are you from? What do you do?

queenofvenice: *I'm Shambhavi, from Stephen's. I kick asses of asses.*

I: That's a good way to contribute to the society. BTW, nice name.

I was flirting with a complete stranger for the second time in my life. The first time was when I was seven, and I received a tight slap on my cheek in reciprocation which eventually made me a wimp.

queenofvenice: *Indeed. So, how many people have you slept with?*

Shocker! Totally unexpected question! I got a little frenzied.

I: *Is it a part of your hardcore feminist survey?*

queenofvenice: *No, it isn't. Answer me.*

I thought of playing a gimmick.

I: *Ummm...one...two....three...four-five...umm....in total 24.*

queenofvenice: *Bloody slut! I knew you would be so. When did you lose it?*

I *(trying to act innocent): What are you talking about?*

queenofvenice: *Your stupid mind, you sucker.*

Pretty brash, but pretty different. Plus, those two pretty eyes were icing on the cake. How could I not take her abuses? A moment of flirtation, a quantum leap of satisfaction.

It took me a while to think of the most imperfect age to lose 'it'.

I: *I lost that, when I was...17.*

queenofvenice: *To whom?*

I: *To JEE! :P*

queenofvenice: *Asshole. Would you like to meet me?*

Now that was weird. Firstly, she hates me. Secondly, she abuses me. Thirdly, she wants to meet me. I was dead nervous. She seemed to be one of 'those' kinds, if you get 'bonded' to what I mean.

I: *Not now. I'm sleepy.*

queenofvenice: *Tomorrow?*

I: *But why? I mean why do you want to meet me? You hate me. You are a hardcore feminist and as you've realized, I am a misogynist. And lastly, you think that I'm a slut.*

queenofvenice: *That's why.*

I: *You're acting like one.*

queenofvenice: *I'm not. I'm not acting.*

I read the last line twice. My jaws fell down and my eyes were transfixed to the computer screen. I was shivering. I couldn't reply.

queenofvenice: *Check out my pictures.* [hyperlink]

I clicked on the hyperlink. Her pictures opened. Seeing them, my mind was completely blown. I'd never seen anything like that ever before. They were shamelessly bold, equally nervy as she had been a while ago.

queenofvenice: *How did you find them?*

For a moment, I couldn't type anything. My mind was boggled with what I'd seen.

queenofvenice: *How did you find them? Are you there?*

I: *Hmm, they were nice.*

I unconsciously typed, still being in a trance.

queenofvenice: *Just nice?*

The word nice seemed to be coming out of the computer screen and slapping me hard.

I: *Who am I kidding? They were full of shit.*

I said, regaining control over my senses.

queenofvenice: *What? Who the fuck are you to say that?*

Her question struck a deep chord within me. I began thinking about who I really was at that moment, when suddenly it dawned upon me.

I: *I'm a hardcore feminist. And I'm against every person who considers woman as a sex-object.*

I used the block feature of my gtalk for the first and last time. I never added strangers to my gtalk account ever again.

Chapter 3:
WHAT'S COOKING?

After both of my books, my readers have asked me the same questions. What happened next? Did Kanav and Tanya meet? Well, I would have loved to tell them the answer, but for a long time I didn't have any answer. I asked them to wait, wait for some kind of serendipity to happen in my dull life. Dull, just because of the fact that the person who brightened my life with her light was no more there. Despite having my love story read across the world, I wasn't able to fix things up to let it continue to have a complete, if not happy, ending. Imagination goes into hibernation when your inspiration gets angry and asks you not to contact her.

The only thing that was going good in my life was my novel. It was doing well, much more than what I'd expected. But, I was still bereft of happiness. Happiness gives you happiness only if you've someone you want to share it with. I never tried to contact her. My mind cringed all the time to break the silent promise that I'd kept to her, but fortunately or unfortunately, my heart had, by this time, learnt to control my mind. I wrote intricate diary entries, dedicated to her, with an undying hope that when we would meet next, it would tell her that I'd changed.

Tanya, if only you'd been nearer, my love wouldn't have been as stronger. Thank you. For letting me know that love never fades once respect is there. Love has evolved me into a better person, a person who has learnt to respect.

I decided that my story would be complete only when she comes back into my life, which I thought to be very soon. I took it for granted that she couldn't live without me. But 2 months long silence without any news from her end confirmed her firmness. I valued her decision. I concentrated on my studies and decided that besides the two week long entrepreneurship seminar in University of Massachusetts, the only way to get nearer to her was to get through a US based job out of campus.

'You know what happened with that Queen of Venice? She turned out to be a slut. She sent a link to her topless pictures to me,' I related to my friends. We were sipping coffee with cheese croissants at Nescafe in the campus.

'Really?'

'Why would I be kidding? She wanted to have a night stand with me,' I said, shyly.

'Now you are kidding,' Anuj slammed.

'Or maybe not,' Aryan took over, apparently in my favour, only to slam me again later, 'after all she hasn't seen his real face.'

They began howling and we walked back to our hostel, when I related the entire story to them.

When we entered our hostel, I showed them the vulgar pics which they relished. I heard phrases like *she's hot, those are big* and a lecherous *naicee*. After Aryan carefully checked whether *queenofvenice* was a fake id or a real one, he realized that it was a real one. He called one of his fast friends in Stephen's and inquired about the presence of a girl named Shambhavi, and he confirmed that she had been there and was quite infamous for her acts.

Anuj faked a call and sneaked out of our room. We knew what he was going to do as soon as he entered his room. He was to add *queenofvenice@gmail.com* into his gtalk contact list and begin chatting.

But, as luck would have it, *queenofvenice* didn't accept his request. He came running back to us and pleaded, 'Kanav, please unblock her and let me have a chat with her. Tell her that I'm the Aryan of your novel, as girls go gaga over him.'

Aryan was flattered and he endorsed Anuj's interest. I declined and said, 'I am not going to do it. I don't want to talk to that bitch again. You guys do it and I'll just watch.'

As soon as they unblocked her, we could see her online, with green dot on the gtalk bar, and the status: 'Turned on, I'm talking about the PC you sucker!'

Anuj and Aryan, with their lecherous tongues hanging out of their mouths, pushed in at the screen. Anuj introduced himself as Aryan and said that I'd told him about Shambhavi and he was very excited to meet her. Shambhavi, being the queen of Venice, didn't take much time and asked him to meet her the very next day.

I warned Anuj to stick to his small town roots and not to go wild in the *Dilli-ki-hawa*, but he rudely said that he was not born to listen to me. I couldn't say anything else.

Sameer and Reva had been together for over six months now. During my last birthday, when we made him realize that Reva had cheated on her boyfriend with him, he immediately ran up to her and they had been together since then. They both had become more plump in the last few months owing to their heavy lunches and dinners together at all the famous places of Delhi right from Gola's to Karim's.

The only good side effect in Sameer had been that he became less philosophical. He became the source of all the raunchy stories going on inside the campus. As he and Reva would be spending most of their time in isolated nooks and corners of the institute at night for their sexual gratification, he came across a lot of promiscuous couples loitering around in the blocks and the institute area.

Once late at night, when he was not yet back to the hostel, my phone buzzed with his number.

'Hello Papa, Sameer this side,' he said. I was puzzled.

'Sameer, this is Kanav, not your Papa.'

'Yes Papa, these security guys are torturing us and even made me call you at the midnight. I was telling them that you knew about Reva and had no problems in us having physical intimacy, but these security guards don't agree to me,' he explained.

'*Saale*, don't you have any shame? You're lying in front of the security officer and expecting me to help. I won't, now see how I am going to have fun with you.'

'Papa, please. I understand I woke you up in deep sleep but don't get angry at me. It's the security guards who made me call you,' he convincingly muttered and said to the security in-charge, 'see, you have made my Papa angry, now you only tackle.'

'First promise me a treat at Karim's, only then I would help you,' I shot my bet.

'I promise Papa, I promise, I would never call you again at night, no matter whoever tells me. Love you Papa, now talk to the security personnel,' he handed over the phone to the security guy, who by then was more or less intimidated.

'Hello, good evening sir,' he spoke.

I acquired a deeper baritone and irritably yelled, 'Do you think it's evening, officer?'

'No sir, I'm sorry for disturbing you sir.'

'Now, I won't be able to sleep the entire night. My tomorrow is totally screwed up, all because of you. Do you know how much I earn in a day?' I asked confidently. I was enjoying the mock play, it being my first tryst with dramatics.

'No sir.'

'As much as you would earn in a decade, dumbhead. Now if I file a case against you for intentionally assaulting me mentally, with my son as the witness and this call recorded, tell me who would save you?'

'I'm extremely sorry sir. What do you do sir?'

'I am a lawyer at the Supreme Court. Now say sorry to my son, before I get irritated further,' I ordered.

'Sir, but he was caught in an intimate position with a girl in the lady's toilet.'

'Who caught him?'

'I.'

'So you entered the lady's toilet?'

'Yes, sir,' he said thoughtfully.

'How different are you from him then? And if I talk about

the law, he was with the consent of a girl in the lady's toilet, while you were not – and with intent of voyeurism – what if I file a case against you for professional misconduct.'

'No, sir that's not needed. Sorry sir, sorry Sameer sir,' he said and disconnected the phone.

A minute later, Sameer called me and screamed, 'I love you Papa, I love you Papa.'

'Son, you are a dick!' I said and we both burst out laughing.

Two months later, Sameer broke up with Reva as she confessed to him that even she liked Aryan in the first semester and thought of Sameer as an irritating fat ass. In her reply, he said that Aryan was gay and all the girls of IIT were gay, to which Reva got offended. Sameer never bothered to pacify her and after much wait, she later apologized to Sameer and said that she didn't think that about Aryan anymore, but Sameer – being so anti-Aryan – couldn't take her back and chose to remain single. Reva with nothing else in hand moved on and got into a relationship with another guy in our hostel, Ishan – the same guy who had once fooled me as a publisher and wanted to read my book.

I asked Sameer why did he hate Aryan so much to which he replied in his classic self-effacing tone, 'for being so fit.'

The treat at Karim's is still pending, and now the fatso won't even give that to me, as he once said that he didn't dwell in the past.

❦

'Anuj just SMSed me. He has asked me to come to Hyatt Residency as soon as possible and pick him up from his room. I think he's in trouble,' Aryan rushed into my room and informed me.

'Why, what had happened?'

'He didn't say anything? He just asked me to rush to Hyatt and bring him back home.'

'He must have been drunk.'

'Initially I too thought so but he has sent me an SMS with no shorthands saying – come as soon as you can.'

'Wait a minute, did you say Hyatt Residency hotel. That's a five star hotel. What is he doing there?'

We both looked at each other for seconds before simultaneously screaming: 'Queen of Venice, no!'

'How could he book Hyatt for that slut? I mean it's too costly? From where would he have got so much money?' We kept questioning each other in disbelief as we drove towards Hyatt.

We rashly parked the car and rushed inside. Before I could stop to notice the ambience of the first five star hotel that I'd visited, to describe in this book, Aryan caught my wrist and dragged me upstairs towards Anuj's room.

We opened the room and found out a horrendous sight. He was lying there naked; his hands were tied down with the bed and a myriad of freshly wounded bruises resided on his chest and legs. His eyes were covered with a black cloth tied across them. At first we got scandalized thinking that he had been brutally raped, but a moment later, Anuj smiled in ecstasy and we realized that it was something else.

The first thing that I did was to hide his teeny-winy under the white bed-sheet, safeguarding his self-esteem. We untied his hands and removed his blindfolds as he sat up.

'It was amazing,' that was the first thing that came out of his mouth.

'But why did she leave you like this?' Aryan asked.

'Her boyfriend came in the morning to pick her up, while I was insistent to drop her off. She tied me therefore.'

'What? She had a boyfriend,' I screamed in horror.

'Yes. She confessed to me before leaving in the morning; she sent Aryan the message when I asked her to do that; that was when she hit me and gave me all these bruises, as she had found out from my cellphone that I was not Aryan, but Anuj,' Anuj helplessly admitted.

'What happened yesterday? From where did you get all this money from to book a room in Hyatt?' I questioned. As I'd got to observe Hyatt from inside, I realized that it was something that would take me at least 4-5 years to even dare to book a toilet for a constipated night.

'*Arey*, you remember Niki, my ex-girlfriend? Her ex-boyfriend works here…'

'You are friends with him?' I asked, shocked.

'Ex of an ex is a friend,' Anuj said in his epic style, 'he arranged it for just 5000 rupees.'

'Just. Is that just?' I cried. He was not interested in answering my questions.

'BDSM?' Aryan asked, talking in his patent pornographic dialect.

'Yes. With eyes closed all throughout, right from when I entered this room in Hyatt till now.'

'Whipped?'

'Yes.'

'Even the other end?' He asked.

'Yes, I never knew that even that could make you feel good.

She had a toy too, probably,' Anuj said. He never felt shy while talking about sex in front of Aryan, his guru in sex education.

'Oh damn,' Aryan shrieked. I couldn't understand what was going on.

'What?' Anuj and I both questioned at the same time.

'It wasn't a toy.'

'Oh damn!' I caught hold of the situation. 'Her boyfriend.'

'Oh no, don't give me that shit!' Anuj shrieked loudly and nervously got up.

We waited as Anuj went into the loo to analyze himself. He came out dressed, and said, 'I can't even file a case of assault. I gave the consent. There was no resistance, hence no injuries.'

'At least you enjoyed both of them,' Aryan taunted, 'you are the first person I know to have a threesome. Congratulations.'

Anuj's face went red with anger but he didn't say a word. A minute later, at the counter, the receptionist came up to us and asked us: who amongst you is Aryan. Aryan affirmed and went away with her.

He came back in a few minutes, his face raging with anger. 'You booked the room in my name and gave my credit card details?'

'Obviously, I'd to meet Shambhavi as Aryan, don't you remember?'

He avenged for Aryan's mockery in a smarter way and I, much like a mute spectator and a dumb writer, adored the receptionist and the exquisitely sculpted ceilings of Hyatt to be able to lucidly describe it in my future works, which now I no more remember.

Aryan rushed to the parking lot and as soon as I got seated, he dashed out the car leaving Anuj behind. Anuj was stunned as he shouted, 'hey!'

'You are not Aryan outside Hyatt, so get yourself what you deserve: an auto.'

Chapter 4:
THE DISCOUNT COUPON

I had been used to waiting but this time wait went a little farfetched. Last time she reached me within a month after the first exit. This time it had already been 3 months and the trouble was that I was too complacent with the attention that I was getting. I always used to think that had Tanya been nearer, I would have sent her an envelope containing the print-outs of all the brimming-with-love kind of e-mails that my dear readers had sent me with subjects like 'Oops! I am falling for you!' so that she understands my value. After the Queen of Venice incident, I was a bit apprehensive about meeting new people.

However, one can't stop God if he decides to fix up divine meetings. It started with a toothache. No not the same teeth that played the role of protagonist in my first book. Apparently, I was becoming wise. Wisdom teeth were emerging from God knows where. I had to meet a dentist. The very thought of the same old dentist, whose ghastly office and skeletal body had once vexed the hell out of me, made my feet run old.

I googled around, found a coupon which gave me a discount of around 90 percent on an oral consultation at Dr. Trehan's Dental Clinic in South Delhi from Rs. 2000 to

Rs. 250. Fair enough. Dr. Trehan sounded a convincing name for a dentist, wise enough to give relief to my growing wisdom.

I booked an appointment via phone where a very sweet voice greeted me and asked me to come on the next morning. I was delighted feeling that there was something to look forward to the next day. Dr. Trehan's receptionist.

The next morning, the wisdom teeth had taken all the intelligence out of me and made sure that I was in no condition to have the early morning breakfast, which was *idli-sambhar* – the only yum thing they cooked at the hostel. I rushed to meet Dr. Trehan, hoping his experience would bring an end to my growing wisdom.

As I entered the place, all my expectations were washed away in no time. I saw an old man with a stern face, sitting on the table, looking directly at me. All my fantasies of encountering a hot receptionist was vanquished the moment his gaze fell over my face and then to my teeth which I consciously hid behind my lips. I went to the old man, told him that I'd an appointment with Dr. Trehan. He didn't say a word and showed me the door. Thankfully, it was not the exit door.

I entered. It was the clinic. 'Open your shoes and lie down on the reclining chair. The doctor would be here in 2 minutes.' The old man shouted from outside. I lay down. My eyes revolved noticing what seemed to be quite well-equipped modern clinic. As I continued exploring, my eyes got stuck at a point, it was a photograph. An old man with his daughter. It seemed like the old bald man had quite a darn pretty wife to bear him a daughter like that. Suddenly, I heard the sound of delicate footsteps and my eyes couldn't believe what they saw. It seemed as if the beautiful girl came out of the picture.

'Hello, I'm Dr. Trehan,' she said in the softest voice my ears had ever encountered.

'H…i,' I mumbled, staring at her face and comparing it with the photograph like a lunatic.

'Are you okay?' She asked, concerned. I kept looking at the photograph.

'Are you okay?' She asked again. I was brought back to normal.

'Yes. I expected someone older to be Dr. Trehan,' I said.

'Heard that many times, try something new,' she said bluntly, which somehow managed to sound polite.

'I'm sorry but I was not flirting,' I replied calmly.

'This was new,' she said with a genuine smile. It was endearing. It enamoured me until it got covered by a cotton mask over it.

'Open your mouth,' she ordered as she peered inside my mouth. Had I known it to be a lady Dr. Trehan awaiting me, I would have come prepared with mouth intoxicated with peppermints.

She pulled out a machine which made a lot of noise and provoked me to imitate it, which sadly I couldn't, since my mouth was suddenly in someone else's hands, literally. She was denting my molars. The wisdom teeth seemed to creep back inside my gums in fear of the ongoing molestation. I was happy to realize that the unbearable pain that made me restless since the morning had subsided. But there was something that was to make me happier.

As my thoughts strayed in leaps of imagination and the first thought of Tanya struck my mind out of nowhere, my lovely dentist completely washed her off my mind. She leant over me. Yes! It was the moment I realized what the phrase women on top actually meant. Thank God she wasn't anywhere close to Pamela Anderson otherwise I would have died of asphyxiation. Amidst high pitched noise and dental assault, all my attention had been focused on her captivating smell and 'the big and the beautiful' eyes that hovered over me.

'So Kanav, when did you lose your braces?' She asked having finished with her carpentry.

The question was as embarrassing to me as if someone had asked me, 'when did you lose your virginity?' It's another thing that I didn't yet manage to, not even after writing two bestselling novels. (All thanks to that girl in the US. Trust me, long distance sucks!)

'Did you, by any chance, read my novel?' I questioned, being flabbergasted by her knowledge about my name and dental history.

'What? Did you write a novel on your braces?' She questioned.

'Yes...' I said and noticed a wicked smile saying *what-a-loser-you-are* cracking up her face. I immediately modified my answer and uttered, 'actually, the protagonist had braces in my novel. By the way how did you know my name and those braces?'

'About your name: you booked an appointment with me, remember?' She said, didactically.

'Oh it was your voice. That's why it seemed so familiar. But what about the dental history? Oh wait a minute, you are a dentist, I remember,' I said, faking a dumb smile at my foolishness.

She smiled. Her perfect glistening white teeth gave me another reason to fake an only-lips-smile.

'What's the name of your book?' She asked.

God only knows how much I hated that question at that very time. I tried to reason with myself, 'I wasn't in love. I was single.' All ready to be 'asked out' on a coffee by her.

'Hello. I asked you something.'

'It's Oops!' I said making sure that I would eat up the "I fell in love!" part from the novel's name and continued, 'it's a humorous story of a man-with-braces.'

'Interesting. I'll surely read it,' she said. I felt flattered. I stood there gaping at her smiling face when she opened her mouth to say something that I expected would make me forget everything that happened in my past.

And she said, 'Do you have change?'

My excitement was brought down in a moment. And I pulled 250 rupees out of my pocket and handed it over to her. On a parting note, I mustered up all my courage and said, 'I'll be here soon, even if this coupon is not available.'

'Sure you will be. Hope my husband breaks your teeth someday,' she said with a wink.

WTF! She had a husband! I saw her forehead. She had no trace of any *sindoor* as such. I was stupefied. Was I flirting with someone almost 6-7 years elder than me? I hoped not.

'Kidding!' She said.

'Oh!' I heaved a great sigh of relief and flashed a wide grin.

'Oh, you took it for real. Ha!' She asserted. I jumped in joy, feeling so comforted by her words.

'Of course, he would not break your teeth. He is a gentleman,' she said.

I came out. There was nothing left to say or hear. A man of

early 30s, who was sprinkling water in the garden, smiled at me when my eyes crossed with his. It was the most gentlemanly smile I'd ever encountered. I realized who he was. Jealous, in reply I flashed my '36'-teeth smile at him. I couldn't take more. I went out in a huff.

Weeks later, I once again found the same discount coupon on internet. Without thinking twice, I immediately closed the tab.

Chapter 5:
THE AFTER-EFFECTS

'Buddy, a strange thing happened today,' I said to Anuj.

I was in his room to inquire about the lectures, that he had fortunately attended.

'What? Feeling disoriented?' Anuj remarked with a vile smile.

'Kind of. I felt an irresistible attraction to my dentist. I was so lost in her that even thoughts about Tanya didn't make me feel guilty,' I admitted.

'Well, first tell me how she was. Hot?'

'No. Very simple and soft-spoken.'

'*Gharelu* type? Saas-bahu kinds?' He said.

'No not like those cry-babies. She was more of a sophisticated and humble kind of a girl.'

'Classy. Was she BIG?' He questioned, being lost in thoughts, rather fantasies.

'She was married. Now get it back to normal,' I humoured.

'Damn! Married ladies are hot. You found a gold-mine. Give me her address,' he remarked.

'Come on. Your friend is concerned and all you want is to

date his newest crush.'

'Aha! Crush. That's something new.. So what are you concerned about?'

'I am concerned about my feelings for Tanya. I think she doesn't bother me anymore. Which means...' I stuck at an awkward pause.

'Which means you can date other chicks, newer chicks, hotter chicks, chicks, chicks, chicks,' Anuj said and was transported into an altogether different kind of a world. It was the trance that he last experienced when he was first introduced to the words like Debonair and Maxim by Aryan, on the very first day.

'Which means I am not in love anymore,' I continued from where I'd stopped.

'Congrats! That's good news son,' he said in a fatherly voice.

'Which means my first book is no more valid. I should write another book.'

'Ha! You are thinking about working rather than dating, what a geek you have become.'

'No, I am serious. What I had presumed to happen has not come true. I can't cheat my readers,' I said, in seriousness. The thought of the third book swam across my mind and it kept floating until Anuj decided to become the gabby philosopher Sameer for some time.

'It's all because of your singlehood. It's time to have a fling buddy; get laid. Life can't be exciting until you've been excited,' he ended his monologue with an additional stress on the word 'excited'. A wink followed. I remembered about Tanya and her frequent winks. I realized boys wink only when it's something about sex whereas girls wink only when they feel that they have outsmarted the other sex. That's why girls don't wink a lot. I was pacifying myself. Tanya winked more. Yes, she was smarter.

'But why don't I miss her?' I questioned loudly. What was supposed to be a question to myself now incited an answer from the Casa Nova standing in front of me. His divine voice tried to enamour me the very next moment.

'Because you are single. And come on; let me hook you up with a girl in my facebook friend-list. You can't get over a woman without getting over another woman,' he said. Ah, it was fun. Philosophy of perversion is always delightful.

Anuj opened his laptop, signed in his facebook account. His childlike enthusiasm made me a bit curious about what he was going to show me. Just when he opened his profile, he said, 'Friend, you have come to the right guy. I am the one who would make your life extraordinary.'

'What extraordinary thing you possess?'

'I have an…let me find an analogy…yeah, I have an almirah of pretty girls,' he said with a loud chuckle, and continued, 'how was the imagination, author-*saheb*?'

'Bestselling!' I mumbled, hiding a mild laughter.

'See, had I not been seeing the girl that I am seeing nowadays, I would never have recommended this girl to you.'

'You're daring! Seeing a girl, after surviving the last washroom disaster of yours is worth applause. What's the name? Niki, Neetika, Niti, Nikita or Neta-ki?'

'This time it's none of those scary names. She is known as Aaina.'

'Have you ever seen your face, sucker?' I joked.

'*Arey*, it's true. Her name is actually Aaina,' he said. Clearly, he didn't get my joke. I didn't try to explain anything to him.

'Kanav, now see. This is Shefali,' he opened a profile on facebook. The display picture was indeed very pretty. I was interested. No thoughts about Tanya came across for even a single moment.

'How do you know her?'

'One doesn't ask the snake-charmer from where he gets his snakes. They come to him,' he said, winking again. This time Tanya did flash in front of my eyes. The memory of that cyber *flash* tOO flashed in front of my eyes. Suddenly a million dollar smile sprang up my face. Anuj was flattered thinking it was for his snake charmer metaphor. *Dumbass!*

'I had been chatting with her a lot. Looks like a really witty girl.'

'Chatting even after you have found your mirror?' I questioned.

Thankfully he got the joke this time. 'Yes, why should one mind multiple mirrors? It makes one look good,' Anuj replied.

Finally a witty reply. I felt so thankful to him that I intentionally transformed my grin into full throttle laughter that lasted for more than thirty seconds.

'Hey, hey, hey, she is online! What a coincidence,' he uttered excitedly. 'It has been three days since I last talked to her.'

He messaged a '*hi*' to her. We waited for a minute, she didn't respond. He was getting restless.

'Does she talk to strangers?'

'No, but I am not a stranger. I had added her almost a month ago after seeing her beautiful display picture.'

'How did you start?' My inquisitiveness knew no bounds. Being an author, I used to get quite a few praise mails but I could never capitalize on them. I could just thank them for their kindness and that's all what I had been doing in the past four months. I felt like a foolish, dumb, withdrawn guy who had no balls to flirt around with people who were actually interested in me.

'I just sent her a message with one of my best, actually my only one – pick-up line.'

'What?' I was amused. This guy was creative, oh my God.

'Hey, it's nothing spectacular, but girls do give attention.'

'Come on at least tell me what it is. I won't use it. I won't even write about it if you have problems.'

'It's silly. Okay here you go, this is what I ask: *hey, are you in IIT? I feel like I'd seen you in the campus today.*'

'Daaaaaaaaaaaaaaaaaaamn!' I screamed so loudly that a couple of guys from the neighbouring rooms came to check whether it was a human or a dog that yelled.

'Hahahahaha,' I couldn't restrain my laughter. 'This ought to go into my book. It's like Sindbad's lamp – it's the genie that gets you every girl, isn't it?'

'Yeah, generally they reply saying: "sorry, I'm not. But I am really interested to visit IIT. You are from IIT, isn't it?" and thus ice breaks easily.'

'Awesome. You're a genius my friend. You should become a love guru, I'm serious.'

A sound that resembled uncorking of a champagne bottle struck our ears. It was Shefali.

Shefali: Hiiiii, sorry was not at pc.

Anuj: Hey, it's perfectly okay. How have you been?

Shefali: I have been fine.

Anuj: What are you doing right now?

Shefali: Nothing, just made a fake account to assault a self-obsessed asshole. :D

Anuj: Haha, who's that guy, let me know. I would teach him a lesson as well, give me the access to the fake account.

Shefali: Leave it, let me do it.

Anuj: Arey, we'll have fun together. I've my friend here as well who, you know what, is a bestselling author.

Shefali: Wow, say my hi to him. I have to go now, if you can please login with this id: jeetendrasinghdhaliwal@omail.com and password: *assholiness*. There is just one guy there. It's my friend's id. Please abuse him with all your might.

Shefali went offline.

We were a little bit confused. Anuj immediately logged off his account and logged in with the respective id. When the profile opened, Anuj's jaw dropped and he didn't speak for the next five minutes. It was Shefali and Anuj was the only guy in the list. In rage, Anuj logged off, signed into his account. Shefali was online.

Anuj : What are you up to? You could have told me that you didn't like me.

Shefali: I like you, son. Of a bitch. :P

Anuj: Mind your language, bitch! Get lost.

Shefali: BTW, before I get lost, let me tell you that my real name is Jeetendra Singh Dhaliwal and I'm from Punjab. Balle Balle! Thank your friend Aryan. :D

Had I been writing a 3rd grade adult novel, I would have loved to describe what I'd heard thereafter. If Hindi lexicographers were to come up with a dictionary for Hindi expletives, they had the perfect person to consult. The rant didn't stop and it went on until it encountered the target. Aryan, upon hearing the illicit character sketch by his pupil, felt so elated that he jumped forward to hug him. 'Congrats! You've become a man, finally. So how was Shefali, enjoyed the *balle balle*?'

I was not to get wooed by Anuj's bizarre plans and random *balle-balle* kind of facebook friends. I wanted somebody classy for me. The newly found out author ego had pumped up my confidence enough to go to the right guy. Aryan.

Aryan most of the times during the second year would be found on the football ground. He had made it to the Institute team and was one of the prolific strikers they had. His flawless physique used to attract a lot of girls wherever he went to play, and after every match, some girl from the crowd would walk up to him and try to solicit him. But he was very particular about his commitment to Riya and didn't entertain any of those. With time, he had matured as a person and now handled relationships much more delicately.

His inbox contained messages from so many of his female fans, that it even outnumbered my female readership. I realized, much like Anuj had realized long back, that he was the guy who would get me introduced to the right girl.

'I want to go on dates,' I'd luckily caught Aryan in his room in the evening. As soon as I saw him, I rushed to him to clear my doubts.

'What happened to Tanya? With a girlfriend like that, why

would you even think about going on dates?'

'She is gone. Don't talk about her. I'm no more interested in her,' I said.

'Wow, anger,' he taunted. Aryan had this strange obsession of catching hold of extreme behaviour and mocking them. Though his Sylvester Stallone look quite complemented his mockery, but the person receiving it at the other end – most often I being the one, would feel conscious and lose hold of that extreme emotion in a moment.

'I visited a dentist recently and I realized that I'd fallen out of love of Tanya because I got very attracted to her,' I said putting a stupid smile on my face.

'Wow, Bajaj is *khushmijaj*. Thank you thank you,' he kept his silly jokes on.

'So tell me what kind of girls do you want? A blonde, brunette or Chinese?' He sat like a broker and started counting the currency notes that was kept on his table.

'I want an Indian girl, who is not too tacky but someone out of my league.'

'You have it, sir.'

'I met this girl in Amity. His father is a millionaire and she has just gone through a break-up. She is interested in mingling. And the good thing is she is not pompous or dumb, like most other bimbos in Delhi. Last night she'd called me to check whether I wanted to go on a coffee with her, which I had to decline. But you can capitalize.'

'Wow, what's her name?' I asked.

'"Shraddha. Shraddha Sharma." This is how she would tell her name.'

Chapter 6:
THE CACOPHONOUS SYMPHONY

Date 1

'Shraddha. Shraddha Sharma,' she said. I can't express how hard it was to restrain my laughter at that moment.

'Kanav. Kanav Bajaj,' I imitated her style of introduction and shook hands.

Hidden in between thick layers of cajole, her big, dark brown eyes twinkled.

She had come to pick me up at the IIT gate on her Honda Accord. She was driving it herself. It was the first time that I was seated in a car that cost greater than 10 lacs. The car smelled of her, a fragrance that had a seductive effect in me. I was awed, more by the luxury being offered than by her charm.

'So Kanav, Aryan told me that you are also an author. Well, that's so amazing! Super-talented, hmm?'

'It's just a time-pass.'

'Wow, now modesty,' she said. I blushed, having nothing to answer her ongoing flattery. For a while, an awkward silence prevailed, when she realized that something was missing in the car. Music.

'Do you like Western Classical?'

Right from the childhood, I had grown up listening to

Indian music – Indian classical, ghazals and bollywood hits. At IIT, the only music that I was exposed to was rock and metal. I didn't even have any idea about what Western Classical sounded like. As you would not expect, I answered exactly the opposite.

'Yes, I love it.' After all, I liked the luxury and didn't want to disappoint the lady who owned it.

She played a symphony by Beethoven on her car stereo. Having no exclusive taste for Western Classical, I started swaying my head according to the tune as she drove towards a mall in Saket.

'You know, I absolutely love this part,' she said and then began the torture.

She started singing in a high pitched voice like an opera singer and my ear-drums cried for mercy, but she didn't listen. Her voice became louder as the symphony went forward and at one moment, it was so shrill that I could see the windshield vibrating in fear. Fortunately, her phone started ringing and I got an opportunity to turn the car stereo off.

She talked while driving through her bluetooth headsets and bluffed the Delhi Police at their check post, which we just crossed.

'So, where were we? Yes I absolutely love that symphony. Didn't you enjoy it?' My ear-drums were still sore and only after careful reflection on what I had heard I could reply.

'Yes, you are an incredible singer,' I flattered her with an incredible compliment for a singer with her talent.

'So, when did you learn singing?' I questioned having found nothing to talk about.

'I never learnt it,' she said modestly.

'I could feel that. So, I'm sitting with a god-gifted singer,' I buttered her ego.

'Oh come on, I don't sing that well,' her cheeks had gone pink. I enjoyed the sight and carried on my flattery.

'Let's talk about your books. I heard that it's a love story,' she intelligently transferred the baton of mortification to me.

'Oh, leave it. It's just fiction.' Now my brown skin had turned maroon.

By that time, we had reached Saket and she'd parked her car.

Meanwhile, a very pretty girl, even prettier than her, came out from a BMW parked next to her car. My vision completely followed her footsteps, carried by her bright red stiletto heels in stylu which clanked as and when they kissed the floor. After realizing that I was already with a girl, I turned my head back towards Shraddha, Shraddha Sharma. I was surprised to find that even she was ogling at the girl with the heel. I resumed my stare once again, when she said, 'Sexy bitch,' and I unconsciously replied, 'truly,' when a light of awkwardness dawned upon me.

For a moment, I couldn't speak anything. I broke the lull with a dumb question, 'So do you have a BMW?'

'Yes, my Dad has one. I don't like it. I like my Accord better,' she replied glibly. The bright red stiletto didn't feature in our conversation thereafter.

We went to The Big Chill and feasted on an Italian dinner. I carefully avoided even the mention of the word novel and we indulged in a talk of interests.

Our conversation caught pace. I found many similarities between the two of us. She didn't like wearing nail-polish. Neither did I. I mean I didn't like girls wearing nail-polish either. She liked to read non-fiction books more than fiction. So did I. She hated the idiot box: television so did I. She was a big fan of Apple, so was I – the fruit – in my case, as I couldn't afford Jobs' classy products. She has had a girlfriend. So had I. *Wait a minute? What did she say?*

'Yes. I had a girlfriend. It didn't work out, I found that girl too complicated and too demanding, so I dumped her. I have been single for a week. Now don't be so shocked, didn't Aryan tell you that I was a lesbian and I just wanted a guy for company to help me find my next girl?'

I was stumped. My jaw had dropped and it didn't come back until she dropped me back to the hostel.

'You swine! I hate you. You sent me on a date with a lesbian?'

'You only asked for someone *out of the league*,' he said fabricating an inverted comma in thin air around the last bit of his sentence.

'But, I also wanted to have a date.'

'Didn't you have a date? She would have paid for the big bill of The Big Chill, isn't it? *Arey*, she knows a lot of girls; she can fix you up with many more chicks.'

'She ogles at chicks more than me. Even if she finds a girl who is apparently good, she would make a pass herself on her rather than passing her on to me.'

'Ha! At least you have got a unique experience to write about.'

'Buddy, I want to go on a date to find a girlfriend, not to find stories.'

'I got the perfectly right girl for you. She is Riya's friend.'

'Name?'

'You will find out yourself.'

Chapter 7:
THE WOOFING MOSQUITO

Date 2:

'Alisha. That's what my friends call me.'

I was in RPM, a discotheque in Priya, Vasant Kunj. Characterized by its shady red lights, the loud music and the pungent smell of vodka, it was one of my least visited places in Delhi. The last time I'd been there was when it was Aryan's birthday.

'Hi Alisha, Kanav. Aryan's friend,' I had to be very loud to overpower club's loud music. She was not really pretty, but was quite smart. She wore a micro which ended centimeters below her butts and a tight top which revealed more than what it concealed.

'Yeah, Riya told me about you. You are a writer or something?'

'Yes, I have written a novel. The second one would get published in a while,' I said, flaunting my only credential.

'Oh my God, you IITians are such geeks. Who writes books in colleges, come on!' She dismissed me totally and in a moment, made me feel inferior about whatever I earlier presumed to be my accomplishment.

'Want vodka?' She shouted at me.

'I don't drink,' I said.

'What?' She yelled back. At first I thought that she couldn't hear me.

'I don't drink,' I said once again, this time louder.

'What! What kind of a person are you? Are you a primary school kid or what?' She asked.

I felt bad about myself. That too in front of a girl half my intellect. That's the power of a Delhi girl. I wondered whether it was another gimmick by my wicked friend to set me up with a person completely in contrast to my character. She ordered vodka shots for herself.

'So, how many girlfriends have you had? Now don't say none; now. I don't date virgins.' Once again she made me feel bad about something that I was proud of. *Was I proud of my virginity? Umm, maybe not. Okay, she might not be right this time.*

'I had one,' I said, reclaiming my lost confidence. Five vodka shots were served on the table, the bill of which had to be paid by me. I just calculated in my mind how badly my wallet was going to be affected by the ongoing date. With the figure that popped up in my head, I was not glad.

'So, did you go all the way with her?' She asked.

'How is that important? You have your shots,' I showed my first signs of vexation. I was cursing Aryan all the while for trapping me in yet another disastrous situation. I wanted to run away, leaving her all by herself.

Suddenly, she took out a cigarette and gave me the lighter. Having never held a cigarette lighter before, I didn't get how to operate it at once. Vexed, she grabbed it back and lighted her cigarette on her own, whispering asshole. I wasn't able to hear that but I could read her lips.

We didn't talk for five minutes. She emptied all the shots into her stomach one by one and started getting inebriated. Suddenly, she jumped from the couch where she was sitting and started dancing crazily. She grabbed me along and asked me to follow her dance. I felt miserable. I had no way to escape the misery as my conscience didn't allow leaving a scantily clad intoxicated girl all alone.

'Put your hand on my waist,' she ordered me. It was very awkward for me. I pretended to not have heard her and pushed myself further away from her.

The other people in the bar were passing lecherous stares at her, trying to peer beneath her skirt. Seeing me dance in isolation, a bunch of rowdy guys started dancing around her. I felt really worried for her and cruised myself in between the guys and held her by waist. After seeing me guarding her, the guys got a bit farther, and I, was somewhat relieved amidst awkwardness of being so close to a girl, who I didn't like.

'You have got great lips,' she said looking at me. I felt bizarre: first the smell of vodka was giving me a headache and now her flirtation gave me sweat.

'Can I touch your lips?' She said and moved her face closer to mine. It stank big-time, so much that I drifted my neck sideways to maximize the distance between us. She grabbed my face with both her palms and rapidly advanced towards me and I closed my eyes praying to Lord Hanuman out of all the deities to save me. His chastity gave me the confidence that He would.

Thankfully, He saved me. She blacked out before she could molest me. But there was another problem. Now I had to drop her to her place, in that situation.

I had no clue what to do next. And in times of great emergency, there comes just one name in my mind. The reason for the disaster himself: Aryan. I called him and after cussing him for the first two minutes I conveyed the real trouble. But things were not at all right for me. Aryan was at home and he said that he couldn't be of help. He advised me not to drop her at her PG because her warden would have called her parents seeing her state and just asked me to take her to some hotel. My other friends, who didn't have a car, were pretty useless. Damn my luck!

I had to do something on my own. I paid the bills: the bitch drank stuff worth almost two thousand rupees and I was left with just five hundred rupees in my wallet. I carried all her weight on my right shoulder. I took an auto and rather than risking my life by going with a girl to a shady hotel, I decided to go to AIIMS.

I went to AIIMS, told the nurse that she was my friend and had gotten inebriated. She needed medical attention and while she was sent to the emergency ward, I slept amidst mosquitoes in the waiting hall bench outside. My sleep got disturbed when a mosquito buzzed just near my right ear for a while and I sleepily screamed, '*Hatt*! Bloody dog!' and killed the damn being. The mosquito later appeared in my dreams and woofed twice, as if in revenge.

Early in the morning, Alisha woke me up. I got up, startled. Though she was still under the hangover, at least she was aware. We took an auto to her PG, when she related to me that there was no issue of a warden at her PG. I could have dropped her there even at night. They didn't even restrict guys from coming over. I was puzzled.

Half an hour later when we reached her PG, my confusion

was gone. Aryan's car was parked below the PG. I accompanied Alisha to her flat and pressed the call bell. Riya came up to open the door, in her airy night dress that seemed somewhat transparent. Upon seeing me, she suddenly pulled the curtain with her hands to conceal what was visible to me. As any ideal brother-in-law would do, I immediately closed my eyes, after having a quick guilt-free glimpse through her white dress. When I opened my eyes, Riya was gone and Aryan had come out, in her undies – yes in Riya's panty, accidentally, only to get his butts roasted early in the morning. Alisha joined me in kicking his ass and we made sure that he couldn't sit on potty comfortably for the next few days.

I never met Alisha again. Though she later told Riya that she sort of liked me. But I was in no mood for another night with mosquito dreams.

※

'I am not going to trust you once again,' I shouted at Aryan.

'I'm really sorry Kanav, but I promise this time, you'll really like the girl I connect you to.'

'I don't believe you. You have been playing games with me. I'm not your football who you keep kicking every now and then.'

'But you do look like one,' he joked, failing to draw attention from my side.

'She is very creative,' he said. I paused and started thinking. That was something rare to be coming from Aryan, I thought.

'What does she do?' I asked.

'She paints.'

'What style of paintings?'

'What kinds? All kinds? Landscape, portraits and all.'

'I meant what kind – impressionism, cubism or realism,' I boasted my little knowledge of art. My sister is an artist and has taught me the basics of art.

'You are talking Hebrew to me brother. Go talk to her.'

'Her name?' I got pretty interested.

'Sakshi Singh. She is studying Fine Arts from DU. She is a bit reserved, it would take her time to open up.'

'Perfect,' I said.

Chapter 8:
GREAT ARTISTS DON'T STEAL

Date 3

I waited for 10 minutes before coming face to face with the artist.

She had the perfect body, especially her torso. It's very rarely that I comment about a girl's body as I find doing that cheesy but here, the comment about her body becomes a compliment, since she was actually good – as though sculpted delicately by the Master Craftsman. We met at VKRV, a canteen near Gwyer Hall in North Campus. I'd traveled all the way North from IIT to meet her, a journey that took me around one hour.

The more I thought about dating her – who was as beautiful as her art that she had uploaded on Facebook, the more I forgot about my previous girlfriend. Tanya, though she had been amazing, didn't have a taste – when it came to art and being the brother of an artist, I missed that factor in her. I tried my best to reason why that day was going to be my lucky day and Sakshi, the perfect match.

She was reticent, and I did most of the talking.

'Heard that you are into art?' I asked.

'Yes – been painting since my childhood.'

'I like your humility,' I said.

'Thanks,' she said.

She was all good, but however, I missed a spark in her personality. She seemed a little bit boring. I remembered Aryan's advice that she would take some time to open up and I kept trying – engaging her in a one-sided conversation - interviewing her.

'Great artists steal; good artists copy,' I said, when she said that she didn't believe in painting landscapes since it was mere imitation of nature.

'Hey, that's Picasso's line,' she said, her face shining in excitement.

After around half an hour of one sided discussion over tomato rice, she opened up. The reason was Pablo Picasso. Picasso is often regarded as one of the best modern painters and Sakshi, like every other modern artist, was a huge admirer of Picasso's art.

'I just stole it from him. Great artist steal.' After half an hour of unilateral talks, I managed to make her chuckle and what followed was indeed enchanting.

We talked about art, artists, photography and poetry and got so much engrossed, that I started feeling that Tanya had been a childish mistake in my life. Sakshi was so passionate about what she did and when she started talking I could just admire her drive towards art. Her favorite subject of paintings was feminism, where she brought out different sides of feminism through her oil on canvas. At just 20 years of age, she had one of her paintings exhibited at the National Museum of Fine Arts and she sustained herself financially through her paintings, not having to rely on her parents to support her.

An achievement I couldn't not stop admiring. I thought how proud her parents would have been about her.

She showed some of the snaps of paintings that she had made and they were class apart. I just felt inferior in front of her, as her creativity seemed to be almost ten times that of me.

I asked her about any previous boyfriends to which she blushingly replied, 'Many.'

As I probed further, one of her ex-boyfriends turned out to be one of Delhi's most prominent painters. Her revelations made me feel worse and I realized that when I actually came across a girl way out of my league, I could not dare to make a conversation with her, fearful of sounding insipid in front of her rich taste. The situation half an hour ago was completely reversed, as now it had been she who was doing the talking, while I was being totally mute. I consciously avoided any talks that were about my books, since she read Rushdies and Coelhos of the world.

'Did you have a girlfriend?'

'Yes, I had.'

'Broken up?'

'Yes, three months ago.'

'Which college was she in?'

'LSR.'

'Oh, LSR. I tell you girls of LSR girls are totally dumb-headed. They don't have any passion and all they do during their college days are guys,' she said, to my surprise. I hadn't seen the assertive Sakshi and her new avatar shocked me a bit. Her comment about LSR struck my self-pride like a big dagger. Not that I was an advocate of LSR, but it made me feel worthless about myself: even I was doing the same, that too waiting for a girl of LSR.

'She's in US right now,' I mumbled.

'Oh, was she senior to you?'

'No. Same age. Her mother caught us, sent her to US,' I said casually.

'And she agreed?'

'Yes.'

'What! What piece of shit-headed girl she was? She could not even rebel her mother? I revolted against my family to pursue arts and see now, I'm on my own. I don't ever visit my parents now. She was a useless girl. I'm glad that you are off her.'

I felt bad for her parents. Moreover, I felt insulted. I didn't like her insulting Tanya.

'Leave her. She's past. You're the present,' I insincerely flattered her.

'Of course I would. But I tell you, I don't like people like your earlier girlfriend. People who can't fight for their right don't deserve to live in this planet,' she had gotten on my nerve by dragging the topic once again.

'What was her name?' She asked me.

'Why? So that you can shoot cuss-words on her name?'

'You are getting personal,' she rebelled, for the first time against me.

'I'm getting personal. You are getting personal. Just because you are driven, passionate and rebellious doesn't mean that everybody needs to be the same. For all I know that Tanya had been very matured and sensitive to not hurt her mother and therefore, agree to her demands, unlike you who chose to get cut off from the people who had bought your first paint brush.'

'Wow, you are talking as though you guys are still committed.'

'We are,' I said, paid the bill and began walking away from her, never to look back at her again. She carried what is pretty common in Delhi: pride of being a rebel for no reason.

I reflected on what I'd said. Tanya was single, no doubt. *Was I?*

She is single, I'm taken and, we were committed. I realized as a slight grin surfaced on my face. Still, I doubted my feelings for Tanya.

'Hey but I like you,' Sakshi screamed as I was leaving. Though I was absolutely flattered by her compliment, it was not enough for me to stop.

'Your art is not great enough to steal me from her,' I said, without turning back. Even her perfect torso had lost its gravitational pull to turn me back.

One day later, she followed me up with a sorry mail. I didn't respond, as she once again prided herself for the fact that she never used to meet her parents.

I was not okay. My mood had become really irritable after the last meeting with Sakshi and I wasn't able to decide what exactly I wanted.

I had no reasons to curse Aryan for the last date. Instead, when Aryan came to know that my date had turned sour as Sakshi got personal about Tanya, he immediately fixed me on a date with his school friend, Shivani. He didn't give any information to me and said that it was just a blind date, which was for my good. I had lost interest in blind dating. It was so not for me.

He said, 'this date will help you. Shivani is just right for you.'

I rejected his plea instantly. But then, he pleaded like a child for ten long minutes for me to agree. I gave in, making him promise that it was the last date ever.

Chapter 9:
DELHI BELLY MEETS A CHILD PRODIGY

Date 4: Shivani
Time: 11 am
Venue: CCD, Connaught Place

It was yet another date for me. Aryan had fixed the date. I didn't doubt on the choice of the girl. Aryan had endorsed her enough and I knew from his sincerity that he actually meant that she was right for me. I wasn't doubtful about my ability to charm her either. However, there was something that was bothering me. I had an upset stomach in the morning. No, not like Delhi Belly, but actually, a bit worse. Yes, Prakriti's call. I had taken all the precautionary measures like the last time, but this time it seemed unconcerned. A call every ten minutes, I can't handle a date with that.

And it was time. She was to reach CCD. Aryan had used just one adjective for the girl: perfect for you. I didn't want to miss this date. I anticipated something different, unlike all the blind dates that I'd been through.

A Louis Vuitton purse entered through the main gate, together with its boss. I had seen her before. Aryan was wrong. She didn't seem right for me, at all. I wondered how he could say that such a sophisticated girl was perfect for me. While she seemed to be searching for me, I expectantly stood up and waved at her. She smiled and came towards me.

'Hi, Shivani,' I mumbled.

'No. I'm Kanika. By the way, aren't you Kanav? I have read your book. I really liked it. I have even added you on facebook.'

'Oh, I'm flattered. Yes, that's why I was thinking that I'd seen you somewhere.'

'So, how is Tanya?'

Damn, I hated that question!

'Tanya? Oh, she's fictitious,' I lied confidently. Somewhere the hope that she would date me someday clouded my imagination.

'Oh interesting. Can I have a ...' she said, when Prakriti decided to play a troublesome game of hide and seek with me, and I accidentally uttered, 'yes, shit...I mean sit. I'm just coming back.'

I was totally out of my mind. I could not even think about Shivani, who was hopefully coming to see me and secondly, this sophisticated seductress who was supposedly awaiting a long conversation with me. The only thing that I was cursing was the ineffectiveness of *Pudin Hara* in curing my motions.

I attended the disturbing call as fast as I could and rushed back to my table. Kanika was gone. There lay a tissue paper with the text, 'Sorry have to rush. Call me on 9999xxxxxx', written over it.

I felt this sudden urge to call her right away. But, since I was famous and I was the one who was recognized by her, my newly found celeb-ego prevented me to reach her out immediately. I decided to wait. 1 minute. 2 minute. 5 minutes. The wait got butchered.

Forgetting about Shivani, I started messaging her, just when a small brown wallet landed in front of me. I looked above. Salwar kurta, a pretty smile and an intelligent look, which spoke volumes of her erudition, struck my vision. I was a bit nervous. Beauty with more brains than me, eh?

'Hi,' I said nervously standing up. She took the seat in front of me.

'Sit down,' she said in a teacher-like voice.

'Oh sure, Shivani, right?' I mumbled.

'Shivani Mishra,' she said.

'Hi, Kanav Bajaj,' I extended my hand for a shake, she didn't reciprocate. Awkwardly I asked, 'How did you recognize me?' cautious enough not to sound stupid at all.

'Aryan told me that you have got crooked teeth,' she said plainly.

'Oh,' I said, baffled, 'as far as I remember, I had my mouth closed.'

'It wasn't when you were coming from the loo. You were humming some ghazal.'

I was flabbergasted. How could she know that I was humming ghazal?

'Are you a tantric or something?' I said, scared.

'I am a yogini. I've been practicing *sadhana* ever since I was a child. As a result, my sixth sense has become very sharp. Your stomach is not keeping well. Just say this mantra "*Agastya, agastya, agastya*" with your palm on your stomach, it'll be all right.'

'Agastya?'

'Yes, he was a great sage of India. His name has great healing power.'

I was listening. Enraptured, not because of her aura but because of fear. I did as she had asked. Consider it the belief or sheer magic, Prakriti didn't call me for the rest of my date – or whatever it was.

'Oh…kay! I wonder how come you know Aryan,' I managed to stutter, before cringing.

'I dated him. I was his second girlfriend and he was my fourth.'

Shocked. But I was glad to realize that she was also human. I came back at ease.

'So…' I started to smile until the realization of having crooked teeth struck my mind, when I immediately *sealed* my lips. No, not with her, you pervert!

'So, yes, I broke up with him because I wanted to be chaste till my marriage while Aryan had different ideologies. Does that answer your question?'

'Perfect…ly. You're amazing; you read minds, don't you?' I questioned, with a childlike curiosity. I was fascinated. It was the first time I was meeting someone so different.

'I can, but I don't. It's against the principles of Yoga Sadhana.'

'Okay. But don't these rules make it boring?'

'When you have inner bliss, these rules only help you attain the divine joy, which is not at all boring. In fact it's the most enchanting thing one can ever experience,' she said.

'Divine Joy. Yeah, it sounds cool as well,' I said, weighing the phrase in my under-developed mind.

'So what are you doing nowadays?' I asked.

'I have done Masters in Western Philosophy, Sanskrit and German. Right now, I'm doing a Ph.D on Vedic Roots of all the Languages from JNU.'

'Oh, you're senior to me, Aryan didn't tell me about that. I'm sorry I'd been very casual.'

'I'm not a senior, I'm an 89 born as well,' she said.

'How?' I uttered, puzzled.

'I was a child prodigy,' she stated as humbly as she could.

Damn! I was talking to somebody way beyond my caliber, in the stupid diction of mine; somebody who should have crushed me like a mosquito and thrown me aside in the dustbin. I felt as if I was the biggest loser on the earth. Why couldn't I be in her place? Why didn't my parents make a prodigy out of me? I was awed. And more than that, envied. Had I been at her place, I would have published bigger-than-IIPM ads in newspapers endorsing my achievements, everyday on every page.

Yes, sometimes I even get jealous of Arindam Chaudhari. Hope he doesn't sue me here.

'How did you do that?' I asked, sincerely.

'Do what?'

'Became a prodigy?'

'Oh, it's god-gifted! I passed my school when I was just 14,' she said, not a hint of pride anywhere around.

I was jealous. I turned green with envy. Why the hell I wasn't gifted? I also wanted attention, I too wanted to be a superhero of my school, my college, my city and if I'd Arindam's luck, I would dare to think beyond all those - my country.

'I was playing cricket in my balcony with my servant back then,' I uttered enviously, trying to prove that my life hadn't been less awesome. I didn't tell her that even my servant used to play better than me.

'Haha, you're funny,' she smiled. Perfect teeth: another reason to feel inferior. Her eyes had depth. They possessed knowledge.

'I know how you passed your exams. You read your teachers' mind while writing papers, isn't it?'

'Haha. No. This spiritual advancement has come only later, through regular practice of Sadhana.'

'Can I get some sixth sense of yours?' I asked.

'Sorry.'

'I mean can I get the power to read minds.'

'Yes, sure. I'll initiate you in the process. It'll take you years of practice however.'

'*Acha*, tell me, I can't understand how could you and Aryan fall for each other?'

'He too is a child prodigy. We both cracked our boards when we were just 14. We became more of newspaper buddies, when a TV channel decided to air us together. We started seeing each other.'

Jesus! This was so not true. The person, who was already giving me an inferiority complex because of his good looks and sporting prowess, was a prodigy as well. But, what the hell he was doing in IIT with me? I mean he was 89 born, come on.

'Now this is too much. Aryan had taught you to speak this shit and fool me, isn't it? It's just a plan.'

'*Arey*, don't believe it, if you want. After crossing the boards, Aryan had his own ambitions. Rather than going for a college straightaway, from 15-16, he went on a world-trip on a shoestring budget, pursued his passion of adventure sports and came back, prepared for 3 months for JEE and cracked it.'

Absolutely incredible!

'I can't believe it. He has become such a lazy ass that he doesn't do anything now. Just some football,' I said, intentionally criticizing him despite knowing his talent.

'Wake up early someday. He runs ten miles a day.'

'Now stop kidding me. Tell me frankly, who are you? Aryan's publicity agent,' I stood up.

'*Arey*, I'm saying the truth,' she had this great fascination with the exclamatory word *Arey*.

I got worked up. I moved away from the table, decided to throw some attitude.

'I can't believe. Tell me what are you here for? To boast about yourself and your ex?'

'No, not at all. Let's talk about you. Aryan said that you are a very creative person.'

Wow, I didn't know he had such a positive opinion about me.

'Eh, are you sure he really said that,' I mumbled, trying to act humble.

'Of course. It takes huge ambition, patience and talent to write a book at such a young age.'

'Ah, I wrote it just as a time-pass,' I shrugged. It was my best modest acting ever.

'I didn't think so. I found it very heartfelt. Tanya must be a very lucky girl to have a lover like you,' she said.

'I'm single. Tanya is a figment of my imagination,' I said hesitantly. Lying always makes me conscious, no matter who is the person in front of me.

'Interesting imagination though. So you like to imagine hot

girls in your pastime, right?' She taunted.

I have to answer her in a witty way. This is the only chance to impress her.

'Not really. Especially when I can date them, I don't really need to imagine,' I said and expressed a victorious smile. She smiled back. The joy of charming a prodigious *yogini* had so far been the best achievement with the fairer sex. I looked at her eyes; they were as deep as a sea, with an extraordinary magnetic pull within them. I got lost in them. Within a few seconds, I could see Tanya's image appearing on her pupil. I felt as if I was dreaming.

'So it indeed is your pastime. How is Tanya?' She said and placed her hand on mine. The touch was magical, I felt a shiver run through my upper body and some goose-bumps appeared here and there.

A moment later I was crying. A minute later, I was grumbling with tears still on, 'I love Tanya. I miss her a lot. I can't live without her.'

Crying in front of a girl is perhaps what would be the most uncomfortable situation for a guy but it wasn't the case then. She held my hand tightly and didn't say a word until I stopped my hollering. She was patient. She was compassionate. More than everything else, she was there. *Shivani*.

Once I stopped my cry, she whispered in a very delicate manner, 'Don't worry, she is fine. She is waiting for you.'

My cry had stopped but eyes resumed their favorite pastime. Two heavy teardrops trickled down my cheeks. I felt light. I felt wonderful. Her hand was still on my hand. I took her hand, held it tightly for a while and kissed it gently. I didn't feel shy. She didn't feel awkward.

I stood up, we hugged and I uttered a mild, 'bye,' and

departed feeling more grateful than ever before for what she had done to me. She reconnected me to my life. And that's not all; she also paid the bill for the cappuccino that we had ordered.

I now knew what Aryan really meant when he said: 'she's just right for me.'

More than Shivani, I felt more grateful to Aryan for knowing exactly what I really needed. As soon as I put my hand in my right pocket, I came across a paper with Kanika's number, the pretty Louis Vuitton girl I met before Shivani, written on it. I crushed the paper and threw it in the dustbin, aside. I didn't need any more dates.

Days later, when I met Aryan, he hesitantly and laughingly disclosed to me that Shivani was a dramatist, who he had convinced to fool me. I can't describe in words what I did to his buttocks thereafter. However I corrected him that she didn't fool me but rather enlightened me, when he wailed in pain upon my fatal beatings and said, 'she was really a *yogini* however. I was just trying to pull your leg.' The rest remained a mystery.

Chapter 10:
CRUSHLIST, CHYAWANPRASH AND MOM

My streak of blind dates was over. I was so glad that I didn't have to prepare for any more awkwardness, irritation and I could go back to where I belonged. Tanya's heart.

Time passed by, I got immersed in studies and for the first time, secured an 8 pointer – better than the trio this time, as I studied on my own, and managed to escalate my GPA to a respectable level.

In the meanwhile, I had completed rewriting and editing my second novel and sent that off to my publisher. I had to prepare a business plan for the entrepreneurship seminar in the US, but I was running short of any innovative business idea. Thankfully, a mail from my reader gave me serious impetus to start-up my own venture.

Hi Kanav,

I really liked your novel, especially the way you conquered your fear of talking to girls. Even I have a crush in my class, but owing to my fear, I have never been able to tell it to her. I have a feeling that she likes me as well. Is there a way I could get to know her feelings without making a fool of myself?

I got a brainwave, an idea that I was going to start a

website on. After a lot of permutation and ideation, I named it *CrushList.in* where people could list their crushes anonymously and get to know whether the person they had a crush on, had a crush on them or not. The anonymous listing of crush would display names once the crushes matched with each other. My hostel-mates became crazy (in a positive sense) after hearing my idea and helped me build the basic framework for developing the website, after which I needed to give around one week of hardwork, to be able to publicly launch the prototype – a work I procrastinated to be done during the US trip.

After confidently acing my semester, I went to Indore, my hometown, to pack my as well as my mother's bags for the US trip. Yes, she was coming along with me. All the way to the US!

Thankfully, my mom had figured out her very close college-friend Sangeeta Sen, who was in Massachusetts and Mom had agreed to leave me alone for the first week of my trip, as I went for the entrepreneurship seminar while she went to Mrs. Sen's place. Mrs. Sen, who I used to call Mausi, called to congratulate me and assured me that I was going to have a great time there.

Our flight was from the Indira Gandhi International Airport, New Delhi on 15th May, 2009. Before leaving for Delhi from my hometown Indore on 12th May, I had a great tussle with my conscience while deciding whether to let Tanya know about it or not.

The main purpose of going to the US was to meet her, but with the promise that she'd asked me to make in that last letter of hers, I was not willing to get in touch with her, just to keep her word. But my journey would have been wasted if I didn't meet her. No matter how far we were, I still loved her. Especially after meeting Shivani, I felt that even she must be waiting to hear from me.

After a lot of contemplation I concluded that I would write to her to ascertain whether my hope had any meaning, though I decided that I would not tell her that I would be in the US for two weeks. As far as I remembered, her college had a provision of an internship in the US, and she was going to stay there.

I drafted a short mail. A direct mail that I thought would prompt her to reply. The purpose of the mail was to ascertain whether she had moved on with her life or whether I was still important to her.

Hi Tanya

Before you close or delete this mail, let me tell you that this is not a love letter or an apology letter. I know that you didn't want to hear from me. I know that my words don't mean anything for you.

I just wanted to know how you are and what's going on. This has nothing to do with the relationship we have or had. Don't reply if you don't want to. Cheers.

Kanav

I unknowingly sent the mail from my id and minutes later, it bounced back saying that my email id had been blocked. I had forgotten that she had blocked my id.

I was restless. I made a new id and sent the mail once again. This time it managed to get delivered. Without tirelessly waiting for her reply, I moved to Delhi with my mom in a long painstaking 12 hours journey on train that was surrounded by blabbermouth aunties, shrill crybabies and flatulent uncles. The reply never came. Never.

I realized that my journey was now to be devoted to its real purpose, in getting a prize for my yet-to-be-launched start-up *CrushList.in*.

Despite us being two, we had over 40 kgs of luggage and I feared of being restricted from going further at the airport. Mom had taken two jars of *amle ka murabba* and three jars of *Chyawanprash* for the two week long trip. And as you can expect, I was the one carrying that entire luggage like a porter. Damn Indian railways for not providing us with trolleys.

We stayed at our SP uncle (remember the first novel, the chapter on Metro Station to Police Station?) place for two days and he made sure that I was overfed so that I didn't miss Indian food in the US. My aunt added another couple of kilos of packaged Indian food. Thankfully this time I did not have to carry them, as my uncle had called his driver along with an ambassador car with a red-circulating light atop to drop us at the airport. I can't describe in words how powerful I felt when I sat inside the car for the first time.

Airport officials saluted at us when we entered. Later I realized they were saluting the car, rather than us.

At the airport, I found Virgo sir (the professor who shortlisted me for the summit) waiting for me. As soon as I saw him, I rushed and greeted him. He gave me some last minute tips, half of which I was in no mood to hear. I introduced him to my mother.

'Is your mother also going?' Virgo whispered to me, clandestinely.

'Yes sir.'

'But why?' He replied, shocked. His 'why' was overstretched and quite audible.

'To save him from bad influences like you.' Before I could say anything, my mother had already answered. I shivered in an awkward fear.

'Sorry. I don't get what you are saying.'

'I'm talking about this,' she said pointing towards his pocket. I observed carefully, it had a pack of Marlboro in it.

'Oh sorry, Ma'am. I'm trying to quit.'

'Whatever you are doing, just stay away from my son,' she advised him. I put my head down in vexation.

'Mom, come on. Stop being mean!' I pleaded.

'All the best for your trip. Hope your girlfriend doesn't smoke,' Virgo whispered with a smirk, a bit embarrassed by the recent remark and left.

'Mom, he was my professor. Come on.'

'So what? He didn't set a great example to his students by smoking.'

'Mom, it's his life. What difference does it make to us?'

'He's your teacher. His students take him as a role model, and imbibe his qualities. He should realize that.'

I gave up. I didn't want to debate with my mother. She was always right, but she never took the right way to be right.

My mother, gifted with exceptional bargaining skills, somehow managed to convince the airline officials to check in our overweight luggage without any fuss, rather with a smile.

'Mom, you are a genius!' I complimented.

'I eat *Chyawanprash* daily,' Mom quickly retorted.

'I take back my words.'

Unfortunately, owing to a slight delay due to the bargaining for our luggage, all the window seats got booked and my mother, who was sitting on her first international flight, got dejected. It was Emirates. She desperately wanted a window seat.

After an hour, we were inside the flight. We had the B and the C seats, A being the window seat. There was a blonde lady who was sitting at the window seat. As soon as the flight took off, my mother excitedly peered over the window but her seat belt clasped her so tightly that it couldn't allow her to observe anything.

I comfortably got seated, with my legs stretched along the isle, and began playing with the mini-tv that was there in front of my seat. My Mom was a little bit restless. Meanwhile, a pretty air-hostess with scintillating long legs came up to our seats and asked me, 'what drink would you like sir? Whiskey, scotch or anything else?'

My mother got enraged upon hearing those tabooed words.

'What do you think of my son? Does he seem like a drunkard? How dare you ask him for a whiskey?' she thundered at the waiter. I was mortified, feeling sympathetic to the air-hostess. She apologized politely. I lip-synced sorry to her, which she angrily ignored.

Things somehow turned normal as soon the velvety blackness of the sky overpowered the dusk.

After changing a flight at Dubai, I slept until the morning sun woke me up. Mom was once again leering over the blond lady's torso to see what was beyond the window. The blond lady was sleeping with her eyes completely blindfolded.

'When she has to sleep all the while, why is she sitting there?'

'Mom, now don't do anything to her. Please,' I requested her. Thankfully she abided by my request that time.

'I won't. But she should understand that we are the first people in our entire race to be flying to a foreign country and should give us the chance to have maximum fun,' she said in an adorable childish manner.

Moms are always cute, aren't they?

'Next time when we return, we will get to the airport early and grab a window seat each. What do you say?'

'Yes,' her excitement was quenched.

We landed in US. As had been decided, Sangeeta Mausi was to come down to the airport to pick my mother up, while Anuj was going to pick me up and take me along to his brother's place, for a day, before I left for the University, which was very near from their house. I was *very hopeful* that at least one week later after being acquainted with the new country, my mother's excitement would fizzle out a bit. Okay, not very hopeful.

Chapter 11:
NEW YORK CITY: THE CITY OF TOYS

It didn't exactly look like what I'd seen in television. It had many things other than coffee shops with idle friends, who would make you laugh. We had just stepped outside the airport and Anuj and I had boarded a bus to a nearby market place, where his brother was going to come to pick us up. As we waited, we began to explore.

I was totally plundered of words upon seeing the beauty of the place. It was 8 pm at night and the lights made it brighter than even the sunniest days back in my town. There was so much rush all around, the hustle, the rapidly moving vehicles, the clanking of footsteps, the aroma of scents that the women carried on their shoulders and the serious look on their faces, as though they were going for their jobs, so late.

One common feature among all of them was that they all looked busy. It's ironical that this country gave birth to the most popular TV series of all time, Friends with all the idle characters. But NY that I saw was entirely different, where people were so busy that they didn't even bother to look at Jennifer Aniston's poster hung on the lingerie shop next to us.

'And they call us IITians, geeks, huh?' I halted Anuj's concentration spell at the pink strap tightened on Jennifer's back.

'Hmmm.' His eyes didn't sway.

'Should I call Ross to make you taste his *feet*?' I said the famous Friends' dialogue, imitating the character Ross' style of stressing the last word.

'Oh, call whoever you want. I'm going to take her along with me. By the way, I don't think she is Jennifer Aniston.'

'Come on, it's her,' I mentioned. He remained unfazed. However a call disturbed his meditative trance, and I inwardly, thanked the call for it gave us a reason to move ahead.

I wasn't exactly looking for a warm reception but it seemed that the small-towned friend of mine, Anuj, had an Oriya brother residing right there, in New York. And we had to wait for him for another half an hour near the same lingerie store named *Eternity*, with red lights around it. Incapable of bringing either Ross or Brad Pitt, I decided to do something on my own.

'I would rather choose to visit inside and get you a pair of bikinis so that your eyes take rest and let your sense of feel get to work,' I said and disappeared inside the bikini shop.

What followed was more embarrassing than being ridiculed for peeing in your pants in your class 2, in front of your only crush of school, a real life experience that induces perspiration in me even to this date.

What seemed to be a lingerie shop turned out to be a shop for all the x-rated things you could find in this world! Anuj followed and his gaping mouth forgot how to close itself, for what seemed to be *eternity*. It seemed as if he had been asked to sing while getting electrocuted. The pink-world was no more a part of fantasy or the hard disk spaces of the laptops hidden inside our bags; it was right in front of us. Implicitly expressed, we saw pumpkins, we saw plugs, we saw some baby dolls and we also observed leathery belts, which if hit with could leave lasting impressions on our bodies. The mere thought of those things brings shiver to my body while I'm writing.

I reflected upon the look on the faces of people who were crossing by me and the red towering lights all around. *Damn*, I was in a red light area. Incidentally, all of those busy faces were indeed going for 'jobs'.

Anuj, trying to be a smartass since his birth, started filming the store with his mobile camera stealthily. Just a minute passed and I could sense something worse coming ahead, when the shopkeeper summoned us. I knew it was Anuj, who was going to get us beaten by those very hunters which hung on my left. We went up to him; I looked up at Anuj and expressed my disgust with my look, in a way reprimanding him for his insolent action.

'Are you guys new to US?' He asked, smiling sheepishly. It took me a while to decipher his accent.

I expected something harsh, but he was on an altogether different note. Something seemed fishy. I tapped my feet on Anuj's feet asking him to handle the guy. But, much like every true friend, he remained mute passing on the difficult baton to me.

'Yes,' I mumbled.

'Are you guys adults?'

'Yes. Umm, may I know why?'

I expected an answer that sounded like: this shop is only for adults, but what followed chilled my bones.

'Would you guys act in a movie?' He prompted, now his smile had carefully subsided. He was talking business.

'Movie, wow! What's it about?' Anuj, who wasn't yet over filming his own movie of the shop, got super-excited about the offer.

'Let me warn you guys, that it's not the general kind of movie that I'm talking about,' the man re-asserted. We both got the clear idea. However, Anuj had some more curiosity left.

'How much money will you give? Give us a quote and we would decide,' Anuj shot the question across. I was flabbergasted. He was even thinking about it. I kicked hard on his leg, which he ignored with a little grunt.

'100$ for one hour of performance,' he offered.

'That's peanuts. We would get better deals than this in India,' Anuj carried on. I was on the verge of fainting.

'400$. Final offer. We don't offer more than this for threesomes.' The American guy uttered in a no-nonsense tone. Threesome! I wanted to run away, yes, I was so damn scared. But more than that, I wanted to take Anuj along with me, who would otherwise be making waves in the Naughty America videos across the world.

'Wow, threesome. Two on right, two on the left,' Anuj said.

'One on right, one on the left,' the shopkeeper's assistant corrected Anuj.

'I was not talking about that,' Anuj winked. The assistant smirked, as though admiring Anuj's knowledge about threesomes. 'Very sharp Indian,' he complimented Anuj.

'400$ deal?' The shopkeeper asked. Now, Anuj too stumbled. The game had been too much for him as well. He said, confidently, 'First show me the two lucky ones.' Even I became curious to witness whether the offer was worth it or not.

The shopkeeper murmured to his assistant to call the duo. We waited, impatiently. Anuj silently showed me that he had filmed the entire sequence and would be selling it for thousands of dollars; he just waited for the two nymphets who he would reject to close down the deal. Two minutes passed by and two

Chinese women came along with two hunks.

The shopkeeper delightedly exclaimed, 'Here are my gems. How do you find them?'

Anuj exclaimed in disgust, 'These! These are Chinese. What the hell!'

I was glad. The shopkeeper replied to our utter bewilderment, 'No, not these Chinese attendants, these guys – my heroes.'

In a moment, I dropped down. It was the first time I'd fainted. Some minutes later, I could feel some wetness on my face. I was beneath Jennifer's poster, just beneath her legs. Once my attention diverted from her legs to her torso to her face, I realized that Anuj was right. She was just a look-alike of the famous actress.

I questioned Anuj, 'What happened there?'

Anuj replied, 'I rejected the offer, but since you had fainted, they shot a movie with you. See, these are your 400 dollars. Fruit of your hard-work.'

'Asshole,' I shouted and kicked his butt. He later told me that those guys thought of us as a gay couple looking for toys. I was glad that I fainted for it brought me back alive.

'Holy shit. Do you know what he presumed when you said four, instead of two? "Very sharp Indian," Rofl,' I teased Anuj after I came back to my senses.

'I saved you, loser. Go and have threesome with those hunkies,' Anuj screamed as he moved away from me. I could just gather enough breath to not faint for *Eternity*.

Anuj received a call from his brother and a moment later, he arrived. I hadn't asked him whether his brother was a real one or a cousin. But his one act proved the obvious to me. He seemed to be genetically very similar to Anuj, for he chose to greet Miss Fake Aniston with his slant-eyed look first.

Anuj, upon seeing his brother, got so excited that he started racing towards him. But not to hug him or touch his feet but instead to jump on his back and shout, 'Bhaiya!' The sudden humping back on his brother's back seemed a bit out of place, especially in the red light area, where we had just been taken as disoriented.

'Hi, I'm Debashish.' His brother extended his hand towards me, a warm handshake followed. He looked sufficiently old to look like an Uncle, but instead he turned out to be a brother. His accent was still Oriya-Bengali-Indian, unadulterated by the western influence, which I really admired. He took us to his Nissan, which was newly bought and had a *Swastika* sign on its front, which told me that he was quite religious as well, unlike his perverted brother.

'Was this the shop that you had been talking about? It doesn't seem like a lingerie shop. Do you even realize that you had asked me to come in a red-light area?' He chided Anuj.

Anuj just stooped his head down, as if feeling guilty, but I could see a hint of a mischievous smile on his face.

We boarded the car, Anuj in front and I, seated in the comfortable backseat. I looked outside and I could see banners which exclaimed 'Only 100$ per hour' and 'Live Shows, Entry Free for Girls'. They all were surrounded by bars and lounges, with billboards with slogans like 'Beer speaks louder than girls'. New York was certainly way different than what they showed in sitcoms. Beer was the new coffee, and bars, the Central Perks of this decade. (Central Perk is the name of the coffee shop where most of the scenes the famous TV series Friends had been shot)

Jetlagged, I started feeling a bit drowsy and gave way to sleep to comfort my bleary eyes. But suddenly, Anuj found his lost voice and started chatting loudly with his brother, and to add to the misery, the language was way beyond my understanding. The banter continued and made sure that my incoming sleep was shooed away, for the next one hour.

I tried to involve myself in their conversation, by asking, 'What do you mean by *eta*?' to which Anuj replied, 'It means this,' and again continued his blabber. Soon, I got used to the chatter and as the New York City passed by, I fell into the most comforting sleep ever, which too was evil eyed, since ten minutes later, the car screeched to a halt. We had reached the two room apartment of Debashish *bhaiya*.

Apparently, there was a *bhabhi* too, who was too shy at first to come out and meet us, and only after Debu *bhaiya*(as Anuj used to call him) persistently called her around half a dozen times, did she come out. With her shyness, I could make out that she was from a typical small-town in India, tied a knot with a person she hardly ever talked to before marriage. Arranged marriages are funny, especially because they are called arranged. Arrangement starts occurring only after the marriage gets over. The *bhabhi* forbade us from touching her feet and asked us to come inside, as dinner was waiting for us.

It was fun; Indian cuisine awaiting us in the holy land of Obama. It's much better than eating shrubs, herbs and 'bush'es that prevailed in the erstwhile past. After the sumptuous dinner, my jetlagged body finally got a chance to doze off. It lasted for 10 hours. 10 hours in the land of my beloved and I was not even concerned about her. The dreams contained fair skinned ladies of Las Vegas and a lot of scantily clad dancers somewhere around my lap, if I be honest.

Chapter 12:
DESI FOOD DOESN'T ALWAYS TASTE NICE

'Aryan had been telling me that you are presenting a really interesting idea in the entrepreneurial meet of yours. What's it about?' Anuj asked me over the breakfast table. And to my surprise, we were having *Puri-Subzi* as the breakfast. It had been 48 hours since I was in US and I couldn't even get hold of one hot dog or one cheeseburger. Not that I'm too fond of all those things, but at least I am fond of boasting about my first foreign experience, which I had none till then.

'The business idea, oh leave it, that's pretty ordinary,' I said, trying hard to sound modest, because I knew that my idea was damn cool.

'Oh come on, we all know that you are creative. You know what *bhaiya*, this guy has written a bestselling novel,' Anuj said and made sure that food couldn't trickle down below my throat. I don't know why but whenever anyone tells about my being an author, I feel a terribly embarrassed. I feel as if the other person is mocking me.

When I once reflected deeply trying hard to decipher the reason behind the embarrassment, I realized that it's the autobiographical exclamatory title of my first book that sent me on guilt trips. And especially, when I am in front of an elder, I think as though they are voyeuristically watching me lip-locked with Tanya, it being the climax of my first book. Isn't it ironical that the situation that made my life hell continues to do so time and again, and it's I who actually immortalized it.

'Oh really, I should check your book on Amazon then,' Debu *bhaiya* immediately said taking out his smart-phone while his face shone in excitement. Voyeuristic excitement, if you consider my views.

'It's not yet on Amazon. Didn't I say that it's pretty ordinary?' I said, assertively this time. Unlike now, Indian books took a long time to get listed on Amazon.

'No, you didn't call it ordinary; you called your business idea ordinary,' Anuj retaliated. Debashish *bhaiya's* face once again shone in delight, as though he was a vile angel investor eager to grab me in his cage.

'Maybe I can help you out in structuring the business side of it. I have just completed my MBA from Wharton,' Debashish *bhaiya* said, with a hint of self-pride. Just then I saw the shy *bhabhi* popping her face out of kitchen, as if hinting me with pride that despite being so bashful, she managed to grab a pretty big fish, maybe after truckloads of dowry.

'Umm…okay, sure. That's amazing! MBA from Wharton is every IITian's dream nowadays,' I complimented, trying my best to maneuver the topic of discussion to something that would not seem like a stress interview to me.

'But hardly few get through,' Debashish *bhaiya* climbed up the ladder of self-praise. His fingers moved close to his face, as though he wanted to pull his imaginary moustache up.

'True. I think I should pack up for MIT, it's getting late,' I said stressing upon the three lettered Mecca for all the engineers: MIT. Though my summit was at the University of

Massachusetts (UMass), which was no way in the league of the mighty MIT, I thought that letting Debashish *bhaiya* know that even I wasn't somebody ordinary was necessary. He wasn't impressed. A moment later, I got the reason. When his dumb brother Anuj could get an internship there, the place was not exactly worthy of getting his eyebrows climb up in awe.

'Two minutes doesn't make you late. Tell me about the idea,' he asked, sounding more like a bullying college senior eager to rag me.

'Okay,' I said, forcing a smile on my dejected face, and began my monologue, 'the idea is called CrushList. We had all been to colleges...' I mumbled in between, thinking whether the shy *bhabhi* had ever been to college, but the eagerness on her face as she was standing on the kitchen door, sparked my interest once again.

'We had all been to colleges and we all have had crushes. But only a few of us, with exceptional courage, had managed to confess to our crushes that we liked him/her during the college-time, but what about the rest? Just because some remained shy, why should they lose the one they like but could never convey? That's where CrushList comes, where you can login and anonymously select your five crushes in the descending order. And send a request to all your friends of opposite sex. They do the same, and if both of your crushes match, it becomes visible and the shyness barrier is broken since both *bhaiyaji* and *bhabhiji* get to know each other,' I could see *bhabhi* seemingly pleased with me and convinced that it was indeed a million dollar idea.

'What weird sort of idea it is? That is going to spoil our culture. Students are not supposed to date in colleges, they are there to study and do research,' the *bhaiya* squeaked. I didn't expect that. I looked at Anuj, in desperation. Mute, he drifted his vision towards the ceiling. I thought maybe the silent *bhabhi* would come to my rescue, who looked quite interested while listening to my idea. But there was a clear dejected look on her face, after what had happened. When my eyes crossed hers, she hid her face behind the kitchen's wall, as if telling me that in their home, it was only his husband who was right.

'I told you it was ordinary,' I exclaimed, in an irate tone, and excused myself from the table.

Anuj followed me in my room, while I was packing my bags.

'Hey, I'm really sorry. My brother is a little old-fashioned,' he tried to pacify me, which was of no help to me. I wanted to punch his brother on his face and kick his *what-I-say-is-the-only-right-thing* attitude you know where.

'I was thinking about telling your *bhaiya* about how well you are upholding the culture, by dating, flirting and stalking every girl on this planet. Why shouldn't I show him the film that you made in the adult store? I am sorry to offend you but I have a serious concern that your brother might not be straight,' I said, making sure that my polite prick offended him to the fullest.

'Hey, that's not fair. Don't call him names. And don't even dare to talk about my affairs with him. He would beat me to pulp, if he finds out what I have been doing at IIT,' Anuj said, calmly.

'What you are doing is your business, not his, right?' I reverted.

'Yes. I know you are right, but you have to understand that I can't change my brother for you,' he asserted, irritably this time.

'If he's so passionate about the Indian culture, what is he doing here in the US?' I continued the fight, even though I realized that Anuj was not at all in the mood.

'You know what. He was the JEE topper of 1999, went to

IIT Kharagpur, maintained an unmatchable CGPA of 10 all throughout his four years of stay, got the Director's medal for the best performer of the decade, and not only that, he even cleared IAS, AIR 4, after which he completed his executive MBA from Wharton – he's the only bureaucrat from India to do so till date. He is in the US to represent India at the World Bank Forum of New York, and two months later, he'll be back to India, as an honorary professor of World Economics at the IIM. And, you are expecting him to have the time to date chicks one-tenth his intellect during his college days?' He said.

For a moment, I got awed. But then I realized there is no use of so much IQ without having even a bit of emotional quotient.

'Whatever. Wish his kid doesn't run away to marry a Nigerian, when he represents India at some forum in Africa some years later. Anyway, I'm going. I'll be living in the accommodation that MIT has provided to me,' I said, making sure that MIT was loud enough to reach the ears of the Wharton-alumnus in the house.

'Isn't it UMass?' Anuj corrected me.

'Yeah, yeah. Would you mind your own business?' I threw my tantrums at my friend.

'Sure, as you wish,' Anuj gave up.

I descended. The *bhaiya* offered help with my luggage, which I politely declined clearly indicating to him that I was not happy. I had called a cab. I could see *Bhabhiji* smiling at me from the kitchen window, when I was leaving. I felt a little bit weird staring at her, and then, decided to look away. Otherwise, the arrogant *bhaiya* might have thought that there was something going on between me and his made-dumb wife.

Chapter 13:
ON THE VERGE OF BEING MOLESTED

The cab took two hours to drop me at the UMass, along with the luggage, that contained assorted almonds, *Dabur Chyawanprash* and *amle ka murabba* among other important things. I had the perfect recipe to win an Ayurvedic Cure Competition, had there been one; but talking about my business idea, I felt that it needed more refinement. I reflected upon the fact that if Debashish *bhaiya* had been more polite, he could have actually helped me since I had absolutely no idea about the financial side of the business.

Most engineering students who aspire to start-up fall in this trap. They don't start a business to make money, they start up to exercise their technical skills, and as expected, half of them don't have any awareness about finance. How can you expect them to have one? After all, they live on loans from friends, juice*wale* uncles and washermen. The only place where they actually spend their money is phone-bills, for calling their better or worse halves residing only a few kilometers away and philosophizing about love, life and often about something else. While those who are the lucky ones – the ones who don't have a girlfriend, invest their parent's hard earned money in cigarettes, poker and often, something else.

All my contemplation vanished the moment my car entered the lush green campus of the University. Seeing *University of Massachusetts* embossed in black on the metal gate erupted goosebumps all over my hands. I remembered reading that one of the professors of the University had recently won the Nobel Prize. I began looking outside, observing passers-by. Surprisingly, none of them looked geeky. They all seemed pretty cool, and some even seemed to be punks.

As my cab was crossing the institute area, I saw a young couple greeting each other with a kiss on lips. I wanted to bring Debu *bhaiya* there at that very moment and tell him that these guys kiss often and that's the reason for so many Nobels; had he learnt the art of keeping his wife satisfied, maybe India would have got another Nobel winner.

I heard the meter's ting and realized that my destination had been reached. The cab halted in front of a Guest Hostel, where I was to be hosted. The mild coldness in the atmosphere, made me tremble slightly as I got down but I was glad to find the hostel to be perfectly air conditioned. I checked-in, the old receptionist made sure that she treated me with utmost care and respect. After getting done with the registration process in ten minutes, I got the key to my double room. Just when I dumped my stuff and jumped on the big bed, the attendant came in and informed me that I was to share my room with a participant from France.

For a moment, I was uneasy, but then the attendant said, 'she will be here in another couple of hours.' My face shone in ecstasy. *She*. I was going to share my room with a girl. A French girl. Wow.

The next two hours for me were really tough. I took out the best of clothes that I had, shaved my face twice, used the most fragrant aftershave that I had. Yes, I carried three aftershaves. I hid all the non-urban stuff like *chyawanprash* and other edible items that I was carrying and went for half an hour hot water bath, where I made sure that all the blackheads on my face had been ripped off. Dressed up, I waited impatiently, as if it were the night of my marriage.

Suddenly, the door opened. An extremely fair girl, with lips as pink as the bag she was carrying in her hand, entered inside. Tall, slender and not at all geeky, she was nothing less than adorable. I smiled and extended my right hand, saying, 'Hi, my name is Kanav. I'm from India. I'm going to be your roommate for a week.'

She smiled and opened her mouth, when my eyes drifted to her teeth. Flood of memories splashed inside my mind's eye, making my attention waver and a flashback of every ordeal that I'd to face because of something that now resided in her teeth played in my mind's screen. A pulse of mortification went through my body. I couldn't look at her any more. My eyes were stuck to her teeth, which were tied in the shackles of braces. Yes, the same kind of braces, which had plummeted my self-confidence to nadir for four long years, which had played with my life ever since my adolescence came into existence and which had taken away the only woman I fell in love from me forever. I realized the reason why I hated myself so much earlier. All her beauty had been washed away from the moment she opened her mouth.

But, a second later, as she spoke, she took my breath away.

'Bon jour, monsieur,' she said in her mellow voice, and shook hands with mine. My eyes got stuck on her eyes and didn't move down. I realized that with a voice like her, braces only added one little flaw on her pretty face, in a way making it flawless in just the right amount. Her slim and soft fingers got completely enveloped in my hand, and I didn't leave them for long, until I sensed a twitch.

She could understand English, but she had trouble speaking English. 'Comment ca va,' she asked. I didn't know what the hell she was talking about and I just mumbled an unclear 'merci,' which meant thank you in French to her.

She closed the door, as she entered. It took me a while to get the hang of her English, no wonder which sounded French to me. After acclimatizing myself to the new sounds, I figured out that her name was Sylvia, she was from Kole Polytechnic, a recognized institute in Paris. She was going to present her business idea, which was on agriculture at the very same competition. Being least interested in agriculture, I showed keen interest and talked about her country more. Eiffel tower, Louvre, Mona Lisa and the stories of Maupassant. France had always fascinated me.

I impressed her when I related how much the celebrated writer Guy de Maupassant hated the Eiffel Tower that he was quoted saying, 'I always have my lunch at the Eiffel Tower, so that when I look at my beautiful Paris, no irritating tower obstructs my view.'

She, all of a sudden, asked me, 'Would you mind if I changed?'

I negated. Why should I have a problem? The washroom was vacant, she could easily go and change. But then something weird happened. She started undressing in the room itself, right in front of me. I thought that she might have forgotten that I'm in the room and I nervously reminded her, 'hey, I think I should move out,' to which she chuckled and said in her French accent, 'don't worry so much. I don't mind. I've been a nudist all my life. Haven't you ever seen a naked girl in front of you before?' She had taken off her shirt and pants. She was in her undergarments.

Scandalized, I just swayed my head horizontally, and stammered, 'in my country, boys and girls stay apart, till marriage.'

'Oh, that's funny. How do you guys *do*?' She said, as she unhooked her bra.

My forehead got wrinkled and my eyes became wider in disbelief. The directness of her question left me totally blank. My ears were still trying to decipher whether her last word was *do* or did it just sound like one. She looked at the mirror holding her breasts in her arms, weighing them and squeezing them. Had it been a movie-scene that I was watching in my laptop, I would have relished the sight. But, I felt really awkward. My legs drew closer to each other, with every passing second.

'Umm…what do you mean? Do what?'

'Leave it. Tell me are they nice,' she ordered, looking at me through the mirror.

'Umm, are you asking me?'

'Of course, I'm asking you, there is nobody else in room.'

'Oh. They are …' I stuttered and could not speak further, when she turned around with those big bundles of joy bouncing right across me.

'They are?' She asked.

'Awesome,' I said, and moved towards the door. If I had stayed there one moment more, I would have lost it.

'Hey, Cane-av. Where are you going? Don't you want to touch them?' She asked, casually. I was in my toughest test ever. How could I tell her that I wanted to and still I didn't want to? She wasn't the reason I chose to come to US, though she could have become one had I been swayed by her. I turned around, perspiring heavily and said, 'no.'

'My boyfriend is coming today. Don't you want to join us? It has been months since we had a *trio*. And don't worry about him, he's cool with both sexes,' she asked me.

Trio in French implied threesome, I apprehended after careful thinking. What followed was a complete blackout. I fainted, for the second time in the new country.

Drops of water sprinkled on my face brought me back to life. But the sight that I beheld upon coming back to senses could have me fainted once again. Her bosom nearly touched my nose and the long brown hair of her armpit poked my eye. Apparently, she was trying to make me sit.

'Wow, you smell nice,' I overheard.

'Ouch!' I shouted and pushed her bosom away. It was my first touch of breasts, and guess what? I didn't enjoy it all. I was scared. Scared of being raped. I got up, checked whether my pant was on the right place and ran away as fast as I could. Even the receptionist got worried and asked me if everything was alright. I was too frenzied to reply.

Had I stayed there for a moment more, I would have converted my business idea from CrushList into something else and my love for Tanya would have been buried in the lust for Sylvia. I banged the hostel door as I left and began strolling through the campus, along with Mr.Up. My heart was beating at around twice the normal pace and sweat streams took more than ten minutes of American cold to fade out. However, I was glad that Mr. Up was quicker.

Chapter 14:
THE RECREATION CENTER

I went for a rapid walk across the campus. I couldn't notice the campus at first since everywhere I saw, I could see Sylvia and her assets. It seemed as though I was still fainted.

Soon, I came across something by the name of Recreation Center that caught my attention. I entered inside, and saw that there was a badminton court, squash room and a big pool table. I moved across them to cross the huge door that lay ahead. When I entered the place, a sudden envy caged me from within. There were well-built boys, girls with perfect figure, playing water polo in a pond like large swimming pool. My eyes oscillated between their full-of-abs stomach and my one family pack. Before the water polo could sprinkle more drops of self-hate, I decided to move ahead.

After crossing Old Chapel, Lincoln Campus Center and Memorial Auditorium, I entered the academic block. Many of the departments, classrooms, and labs radiated from there. If you happen to ever go there, make sure that whatever you do, stay to the right when traveling through the corridor, else when the classes let out, you might be crushed under the stampede.

I entered the library, showed my visitor pass and got surrounded by an abnormal lull. There was not a single student in the library in my purview. I was astonished.

I got myself into the stranded section of entrepreneurship, trying to find out a handy book on finance for start-up guys. I overheard a lot of whisper, coming from behind the corner most bookshelf. Well, after receiving the kind of promiscuous welcome that I received at the UMass, it was more or less expected. A couple was busy with each other. The only unique thing was that it were two girls. I got disgusted. I mean they are of the same sex; they could have done it in their respective rooms. Why, for God's sake, a library?

Surprisingly, the voyeur in me was in deep hibernation, thanks to Sylvia. I began my search and found the book. But my concentration encountered a speed-breaker as soon as I tried to study. The whispers became louder, with occasional moans.

I was irritated. Where had I come? Some kind of a red light area, that everyone was wantonly doing it? Vexed, I went towards the husky corner and faced the two ladies. As soon as they saw someone coming, the noise stopped. They were blondes; one had her jeans unbuttoned, while the other, who was fairer, had her fingers in her mouth.

'I'm sorry to disturb, but would you mind doing your *stuff* back in your hostel?' I said, hiding my rage.

The fairer blond took her middle finger out of her mouth, and insolently, showed it at me.

'Fuck off, you black skinned pea,' she said, in a low volume. It was my first encounter with racism.

I lost my mind. I ran to the librarian, to complain about those girls making out in the corner and passing racial remark against me. The librarian tried his best to sound polite, but in the meanwhile, showed the racial side of him.

'What did they say?' He asked me.

'They called me a ... umm ... a black skinned pea,' I related, feeling deeply insulted.

A sly smile popped up the librarian's face which he consciously hid and said, 'sorry for that. I'll write a complaint against them.'

'You haven't even seen their faces. You don't even know who I'm complaining about, how would you write the complaints?' I interrogated.

'Hey boy, stop questioning me. You do not belong to this University, it is better if you learn to mind your own business.'

'What the hell! You all are bloody racists. I'll complain to the authority,' I said and made a swift exit. My ears had gone red and blood had already boiled.

Immediately, I rushed to the administrative block and on my way, I saw someone who looked like an Indian to me. Finding an Indian in this critical situation brought in a little peace to my mind that was full of rage. I ran up to him, and greeted him with a panting *hi*.

'Hi,' he responded, politely. We shook hands.

'I'm Kanav, from Delhi. Which state are you from?' I oppugned.

He smiled, and replied, 'Neighbouring state.'

'Punjab?' I questioned, though his extremely fair complexion made him look like a Kashmiri.

'No.'

'Umm, Haryana?'

'No, Pakistan.'

The inherent response in me was not welcoming. He started feeling a bit stranger. I moved a step back, and then realized what I was thinking was yet another form of racism. Feeling guilty, I immediately stepped forward, along with a smile.

'My name is Wasim, I'm from Lahore. I have been pursuing Ph.D. here for the last 3 years,' he stated; his tone as soft as his mother tongue *Urdu*.

'I'm so glad to find you Wasim,' I said.

'You seem worried, Kanav *bhai* if you don't mind, may I know what the issue is?' He said, delicately. I hadn't encountered so much courtesy ever before.

'I have been a victim of racism. At the library.'

'Oh, the librarian? He's infamous for his bad tongue. Our Library is often called as the real Recreation Center. He has made the library into a brothel,' Wasim said, clearly uneasy while speaking the last word and continued, 'nobody goes there nowadays.'

'What the hell? Doesn't the administration do anything about it?'

'No. Almost all the complainants had been from Asians and as you can expect, the management doesn't bother to listen to an inferior color.'

'That's sad,' I exclaimed, horrified.

'That's life,' he said, calmly. I related to him about the experience with Sylvia in the morning. He didn't seem shocked. He said that the campus had been under bad influence for long. 'Every non-Asian newbie here automatically gets dragged into all of that.'

I grimaced. I didn't like what I heard. It made me want to run away from that place. I could sense that Wasim had some work, after all Ph.Ds are not supposed to have a life. After conveying my gratitude, I set him free.

Chapter 15:
LET'S MAKE A TAPE!

I decided to walk back to my hostel, hopeful of finding Sylvia dressed this time. It's strange for a guy of my age that I was hoping to not encounter a naked girl. I was fearful of getting assaulted, if not the body, then at least the gums — she had braces, remember?

I advanced towards the hostel, every step being taken in absolute awkwardness. I looked at my watch. It was evening. All of a sudden I remembered that she was going to do it with her bisexual slut boyfriend and my feet started trembling. I decided that I would go only after the sunset. The dusk had just set in and I stopped near the park to distract my mind with the beautiful sunset that lay in front of my eyes. After wasting some more time in the dimly lit streets around, I went inside the hostel, opened my room cowardly, squeezing my eyelids, as though to push my eye-balls inside my skull, to not witness something explicit.

After I encountered a pin-drop silence, slowly I opened my eyes. There was nobody in the room. *Huh!* I sighed. I hadn't experienced such a relaxing moment in US, till then.

Bleary eyed, I lay myself on the fluffy mattress, looked at the ceiling gratefully, and closed my eyes. I was so tired that I didn't even get to know when I dozed off.

Just when I was about to go deep into my sleep, my bathroom's door creaked loudly and I woke up, startled.

Half awake, half asleep, I looked up at the bathroom's door. I thought as though I was dreaming. I shook my head and observed carefully. There they were. All wet, with towels on their shoulders. Only a towel. They were looking at me. I was, well, I was looking everywhere I could. A loose piece of flesh hung below his tattooed abs (yes! he had abs and biceps too), her pink nipples had hardened. I looked below her waist but swayed my eyes immediately. To tell you the truth, I didn't feel right, though she didn't have any problem. Bloody conscience!

'Hey, we were just bathing, didn't know that you were coming,' she smiled, blithe as a child. I looked at her braces. It didn't mortify her. After all she had such big assets.

'Hi,' I said. For a change I was not nervous. Maybe because I'd realized that I was better endowed than the loose douchebag standing, rather sleeping, there.

'Mark, this is Cane-av, the guy I told you about. Cane-av, this is my boyfriend,' she said.

Mark smiled and waved a mild *hi*. He was feeling a bit weird, as could be seen from his body language. His teeth were more yellow than the dusky sky that I'd seen. I smiled back, flashing my glistening white teeth; another reason to feel confident.

'Guys, shake hands. Mark, don't feel shy.' Sylvia instructed her boyfriend.

Fortunately, he tied his towel around his waist else I would have made him feel bad about his apparently tiny instrument. I shook hands, when he asked shyly, 'Interested to join us?'

'Are you guys not over yet?' I scream. I was utterly irritated.

'We are, but there's always a space for more,' Sylvia remarked, by now, she reclaimed a dignified position as she put her towel around her private area.

'I'm sorry,' I said, politely. By now, my drowsiness had faded away, and I stood up to go out.

'We'll make a movie and make thousands of dollars. Come on, let's make a tape.'

I could not believe what I heard. The thought of a porn movie titled 'Crazy Threesome' starring Kanav Bajaj crossed my mind. I started perspiring. I could sense that my blood was about to boil. A minute later, I lost my mind.

'Are you fucking crazy?'

'What crazy? We'll blur our faces. That's how we make money to sustain our venture.'

'What are you? Pornstars?' I screamed and banged the bathroom door hardly.

'Man! We are just lovebirds. Sorry to have asked you, you Indian swine.' Mark yelled.

I could not control myself. I could not tolerate bringing India into all this. With all my force, I smashed his balls with my feet beneath his towel, shouting, 'I'm not your lovebird, you European swine!' I chose to not insult his country.

A loud scream followed and he crumbled into the ground. Sylvia couldn't believe what had happened.

'Lady, get dressed, otherwise I am going to call the police,' I warned Sylvia. Terrified, she got in her undies and rushed to Mark, asking him whether he was alright.

I packed my stuff and exited their room. Just as I stepped out of the room, I remembered that I had forgotten something. I knocked and steered my neck inside the door, and uttered softly, 'I'm sorry,' and rushed to the warden.

Luckily, warden's assistant was another Pakistani, Zaffer, and he turned out to be a huge help. He gave me a single room, asking me not to tell it to any other participant or the warden. I couldn't thank him in words and took him out for a dinner, where fortunately the flesh of chickens replaced the flesh of chicks.

Chapter 16:
WE PREVENT LOVE LOSS

The next morning was a busy one. Every participant had a mentoring session with noted entrepreneurs and investors of the Silicon Valley. In case you don't know about the Silicon Valley, just know this fact: it's not the place where Pamela got blessed.

I had three mentor meetings scheduled, one with an angel investor by the name James Ruckus, another with an IT entrepreneur whose name I just forgot and the third one with an Indian lady, Devyani Padmanabham who was a professor of Business Studies at Indiana University.

The meetings with the first two guys were very meaningful; they gave me a lot of insight into how to see the business side of Crush List. They liked my idea and also gave the green signal to launch the beta version of the website that I'd privately built. Both of them asked me to get the answers to the first question right: How would I get to one million users immediately?

After a lot of brainstorming, I came up to the essence that the idea had to be inherently viral. The users should bring more users, and one of the key ways to do it was to integrate it with facebook, so that people could tag their crushes and they could get notified from the application.

It took me four hours of brainstorming, eight cups of black coffee and one intense argument to get my business plan right. The best part was that they were very motivating and they both had high regard for Indian entrepreneurs, as Ruckus said, 'No one can beat an Indian, who is driven.'

The third meeting, however, went in the exactly opposite direction. Devyani Padmanabham, M.Sc. Economics from London School of Economics, and a Ph.D in Business Administration in Start-ups from the University of Columbia, as it was mentioned in her business card, had a great detachment with the country where she was once born.

'Hello Madam, I'm Kanav, from Indian Institute of…' My greeting to Devyani was stopped in the mid-way.

'Hey, I'm not here to listen to the introduction of your outdated institute. Talk business,' she asserted. I was reminded of my grade 1 teacher, who used to beat us with a rod, every time we disturbed the pin-drop silence of the class.

Nervously, I took out my business plan, opened it in front of her, waiting for her perusal.

'What? What should I do about this voluminous junk of papers?' She oppugned and winced irritably. She was in a real bad mood. Either she had a fight with her husband or she had met some participant who was worse than I was, prior to my turn. The latter seemed more feasible and made me feel better as well, so I chose to go along with that presumption.

'Sure, let me explain,' I said, gathering all my courage.

Fortunately, this time she didn't interrupt. I began and completed the elevator pitch of my idea in one go.

'Interesting idea,' she said. At first I could not believe what I heard. She knew how to say something positive.

'But there is no future,' she asserted. Her voice was so confident that at first, I wanted to burn the pile of papers that carried my business plan and pursue whatever she wanted me to. If she had told me to drop out of my college and sell chewing gums, I could have given it a thought at that moment. But fortunately, after a minute of assimilation, sense prevailed.

I questioned, 'how can you say that?' It was the first time I brought her into the hot seat.

'Because it's an idea made for the US audience. And as I can see from your face, you want to start it in India,' she said, subtly bringing sarcasm in her voice, which I could only realize few seconds later.

'How can you say that?'

'I have been born and brought up in India, having spent over 25 years there. You think you know more about India and Indians than me?'

'Absolutely not. You are wiser. All I'm asking is how could you say that my idea won't work in India?'

'Because having crushes, falling in love and all that jazz are mythical concepts in India.'

I inwardly smiled. I knew that now it was my turn to charge her.

'When had you last been to India?' I questioned, my eyes digging hers.

'Ummm...late 90s.'

I got shocked. That woman despised India and thought ill about it based on her extreme opinion formed as early as 20 years ago. That's like the age of dinosaurs, on TV, of course.

'And you think that the India of your first 25 years hasn't

changed at all in the last decade?'

'Ummm, no. But I can bet that the thinking wouldn't have changed.'

'Let me show you something, in this voluminous junk of papers,' I took out my sidelined business plan, opened the participant's profile sheet and asked her to read my bio.

She carefully read, vocalizing everything she went through.

Kanav Bajaj is a student of Indian Institute of Delhi and the author of the bestselling book 'Oops! 'I' fell in love!' which has sold over 50000 copies.

'So, things have changed. People are reading about love, hmm?' She asked.

'They are not only reading. But they are doing it even,' I winked, hoping to extract a smile out of the irate lady. She didn't smile.

Being a writer, I sensed her tragic story. I intentionally said, 'Had you been in India now, you could have married your beloved. Parents have become cool.' Despite the fact that the last bit about parents turned out to be absolutely false, in my case.

She coughed. She tried to drift from the topic I raised, but I didn't let her do so. I said, 'Use *CrushList.in*; it works even for long lost Indian crushes,' and walked away from her table with my business plan, which suddenly started seeming very bright. I left one of my business cards on the table.

I turned back to catch one last glimpse of her. She was going through my business card, which carried the tagline that I had devised for CrushList: 'We prevent love loss!'

I returned so motivated that I didn't want to relax at all. I went back to my single room and went through my entire business plan once again. It inspired me to work harder.

I took out my laptop and began doodling with the codes. The basic prototype – the website, which hadn't yet been launched to the outside world, was ready and I just amalgamated the suggestions that the mentors gave me. Two days later, there was the business plan competition and as advised by my mentors, I realized that I'd to fetch some users quickly.

Without wasting a lot of time, I immersed myself into coding. Having already created the prototype, it took me four hours at stretch to fix the bugs and make things public. The website was up and running. I wrote a mail and sent it to all my batchmates and friends, approximately 500 in number, and included Anuj's brother as well, with his wannabeish email id: debashish_wharton@ymail.com (as told by Anuj).

Dear friends,

Good news! The project that I was working on is ready for the first launch. It's called CrushList, and can be accessed at CrushList.in

This is going to prove to be a boon for all the shy people who can enlist their crushes and an anonymous mail gets sent to their crush, which says that they are someone's crush. They come and enlist their crushes to find out who's the real one.

So, your name is not disclosed until your crush comes to the website and enlists you as his/her crush. How wonderful is that?

P.S. Do report bugs and anything that you think would make the user experience better.

As soon as I sent the email, people started flooding on my website. I received 100 hits within the first hour. In the second hour, the number crossed 300. By the third hour, it had crossed 800. It was going viral. People were listing their crushes. I scanned the users; there were a lot of new users other than that from my network. I was happy beyond measure.

One email id sounded pretty familiar. Devyani.Padmanabham@ymail.com. I listed her as my crush, just to send her an anonymous notification and tease her. She came back to the website immediately as I listed her, finally listed her crush with the email id: shashwat.ojha@potmail.com

I searched shashwat.ojha@potmail.com on facebook and found him out to be a professor of Economics at JNU. His profile picture had a very pretty woman in *sari* standing next to him. I sensed the tragedy in her story. Surprisingly, I couldn't get the sadistic pleasure out of it. I felt bad for Devyani.

I resent the listing notification to Shashwat, this time the mail contained the hint that the person's initials were D.P.

Till then, no crush listing matched with each other. I encoded a new feature in which the site publicly announced every match-making that was happening, to their network of friends, if they chose to make it public. I desperately waited.

I didn't realize how and when I fell asleep. I woke up to the sound of the doorbell: the housekeeper. Immediately I logged into my website and saw the activity. There had been 6000 hits in the first 24 hours, with over 2500 registered users. I scanned my administration panel to see if there had been any matchmaking that had taken place.

After a deep scan I could find just one matchmaking to have taken place. No, it wasn't Devyani. Shashwat Ojha seemed pretty contented with his married life, since he didn't reply – not even till now, though he logged in the website once, in comparison to Devyani, who logged on more than ten times for the next few days.

Coming back to the matchmaking that had taken place, it was a lady with the email id: kakuly_das@potmail.com, and on the other side, was a person with the email id: ritwik_bagchi@jahoo.com. I got curious and traced their locations, from their unique IPs, an act that's professionally unethical and none-of-my-business. But, all that jazz was okay as I had not drafted the *Privacy Policy* for the website yet. I found out that Kakuly was based in New York, while Ritwik was based in Kolkata. Long distance, hmph!

Both being strangers to me, it seemed to be of little interest to me and I couldn't figure out anything spicy out of it. *Until later.*

Chapter 17:
WE COULDN'T PREVENT LOVE LOSS

It was the first time in my life that I was suited. Dark grey suit, with black and grey tie and shiny black leather shoes made me feel like the next Casa Nova in town. Being skinny that I had always been, if I were to agree with Zaffer, I was looking like a brown-skinned Barney, which he called Browney. (Barney is the famous character of the TV show *How I Met Your Mother?*)

'Now be my wingman, friend,' Zaffer said. He was accompanying me to the contest, as we had become quite good friends by then. Anuj was also coming for my big day, though 2 hours later owing to what he said was some personal problems, to witness my presentation to the panel. In the conference hall, teams from each country assembled and represented their ideas. I joined the India troop, which consisted for four more participants from India, and dragged Zafar along with me, since the other participants looked geeky freaks with big spectacles and small eyes.

'It's time to be with your wingman, not countrymen,' I said to Zafar. He complied without any reluctance. Friendship is above countries, friendship is above religions.

Introductions began; the procedure was pretty similar to the Miss World paegent. We were to give our 30 seconds introduction followed by 30 second elevator pitch of our idea. One by one, participants went towards the center-stage, confidently summed up their ideas and came back smiling. Even Sylvia, who was dressed for God's sake, went on to introduce herself along with her boyfriend. Thank God, they didn't start doing it there!

My turn came and I could hear my heart pounding. Don't know why, I was nervous. Nervous of being ridiculed by the elite judging panel. As I scanned my eyes across the jury, I saw Devyani seated there. My nervousness increased, when she shooed it away in one go, by smiling. Yes, she knew how to smile. Confident, I began, and finished, in 60 seconds sharp. The applause that followed still resonates in my ear.

Based on the first round, that had 50 percent weightage of the audience marks, out of 250 teams, I made it to the top 25. Full of emotions, Zaffer hugged me despite the fact that no teams from Pakistan had been able to make it to the top 25. I became more focused.

Now, the individual presentation round was due, which was going to be followed by an intense Q & A round with the judges.

I managed to cruise through the individual presentation round at ease, since I'd intertwined all the advices that I received during my mentorship session into the presentation. I made it to top 8. Now there was significant pressure, since the top 3 had humungous prize money besides being given an incubation offer with one of America's prominent start-up incubator.

Anuj notified me through an SMS that he had arrived just before the third session and he was seated in the audience during my Q & A session. The judges seemed to be in a mood to kick participants' asses. Hopeful that the smiling Devyani would make things work in my favor, I moved to the center stage. A bright spotlight was directed at my face, making it almost impossible for me to see the judges.

'So, Kanav, who do you think the target market of your idea is? What's the business model that you have thought of? What's the team? How are you going to scale up to a million users within the next six months?' and blah blah blah buzzed my years. I answered most of them, though I don't know whether the answers really answered their concerns or not? After a grueling twenty minutes torture, they asked the final question:

'Any successful crush-matching till now?'

'Yes. On the first day itself. A lady named Kakuly Das from New York committed to her crush in Kolkata, India.' I proudly said.

I heard a loud applause, not realizing that I was standing stupidly with a lip-rupturing wide grin on my face, getting clicked by random photographers. I instead felt like a celebrity.

I descended the stage and tried to acclimatize my eyes with the sudden decline in brightness. Zaffar congratulated me at the backstage saying that I'd nailed the American Beauty. I came out of the backstage and I could see Anuj rushing towards me. I extended my arms to hug him, saying drowsily, 'Friend, I missed you.'

He didn't hug me. Instead, he grabbed my hand and took me to the sides.

'What name did you say at last? Kakuly Das?' He asked, his voice cracking because of his vehemence. There was something terribly wrong.

'Yeah, why? Any long lost girlfriend?' I joked, trying hard to soothe his mood.

'Man, she is my *bhabhi*. She ran away yesterday, back to India. I told you that I'd some personal problems because of which I'll be late. This was it.'

'What the fuck!' I exclaimed. My head was in my hands.

'She wrote a long letter to my brother saying that she didn't want the rest of her life to be wasted in living with a person having no interests, and she was going back to India forever, to marry her beloved, who was a tabla player. Incidentally, my bhabhi had been a trained Kathak dancer.'

'A person having no interests. So true,' I gagged. Something tickled me deep within.

'Asshole, it's because of you that she managed to tell him.'

'How did she get to know about my website? I didn't send her a mail,' I asserted.

'My brother had opened it on his laptop, when you'd sent that mail. She saw it then. Next day, she cracked it through.'

'Wow, I didn't know she was a tech-savvy bhabhi,' I said.

'Apparently, she had this huge crush on this guy before her marriage and they couldn't say that to each other. Yesterday, she might have come across the link to your website, through *bhaiya's* PC and the rest is history. She ran away yesterday night, writing a note, that she hated my *bhaiya*. My *bhaiya* is in depression right now.'

'I'm sorry,' I said, 'not for what happened, but what is going to happen now,' and continued, 'Ha-ha-ha!' I laughed riotously. Sadistic pleasure, aha.

His brother had ruthlessly thrashed my idea, and now, see how ruthlessly had I taken revenge, with the same idea that he claimed was bound to be doomed. Now his life was doomed.

In an impulse, Anuj grabbed me by my collars, looked into my eyes in anger but didn't say anything. A moment later, he left me and started walking away, without saying a thing. Surprised, I ran after him and asked him if he was okay. He didn't respond. I tickled him on his skinny stomach until he himself started laughing. Our two-man act must have seemed weird to the world, because I saw Mark approaching towards me with a smile. Before he could ask 'us' out, I decided it was time to run away. I grabbed Anuj's shirt and ran towards my room. The results were to come out in the evening and I chose to relax.

To chill Anuj's mood, I told him about Sylvia. Upon hearing the Sylvia story, he got so much interested that he directly went to Sylvia's room. Fortunately, they were at the Conference Hall and though Anuj didn't acknowledge, it also saved him from being assaulted.

Without Sylvia, Anuj's killer mind got busy in tracing the email id of the Bong lover who wooed his *bhabhi* from his boring *bhaiya*. I lay down, playing *Twinkle twinkle* on the harmonica that I had recently purchased. After much effort, without any help from my end, Dasgupta should be Ritwik Bagchi and drafted a beautiful mail, full of dirty adjectives. He included the deluge of qualifications of his elder brother and even managed to include his, to let the tabla virtuoso know that he could never stand in league with Debashish *bhaiya*.

'Don't you think that it would be weird if you send that mail?' I questioned.

'What weird? She ran away, leaving my brother all alone.'

'Even you dumped your girlfriends. So that way even you should have been insulted by your ex's brothers.'

'What Kanav? You are still a child. There is a huge difference between a girlfriend and a wife. You don't ditch when you are a wife. You divorce.'

I pondered, ultimately having to agree with the thin guy.

'Sigh, sent it to that dog in Bengal. I feel so relieved, though it's not going to help in any way, but still,' Anuj said.

'Good for your brother who has no interests – not even in his wife,' I said, only to realize later that I'd crossed my limits. I quickly said sorry before Anuj could hurl back tons of cuss words at me.

'The reason I decided to come here despite the tragic upheaval back home was I needed another help from you,' Anuj said, in a serious tone, and continued, 'as you might be leaving for your aunt's place tomorrow, I would not get a chance to meet you.'

I got inquisitive. 'You are killing me. Stop hiding the suspense like saas-bahu serials. Tell me the damn thing!'

'I like a girl.'

'What? Didn't you have a girlfriend back in India?' I shrank back in disgust.

'I broke up with her. There is a girl interning in the Economics department, next to mine. I saw her at the coffee shop. She is Indian. I have heard her friends call her Tanu. That's all I know,' he said.

'What do you want from me?' I said, wincing at him.

'I want to ask her out on coffee tomorrow and I want to cast a lasting impression on her. Bro, her name is four lettered. My name is four lettered as well. I would do anything for you if you could make an ambigram for me?'

'Anything?' I asked.

'Yes, of course.'

'Tell your brother that you think that CrushList rocks!'

'No way. Not at all.' There was a severe jerk in his body, reflecting awkward fear.

'Well, no way to your ambigram.'

'This is not done. Okay, I'll tell him.'

'Not will, but now. Call him and tell.'

'This is so not done. You are blackmailing me.'

'This is so much done. After this entire long wait, I get a chance to blackmail you.'

He took out his cellphone, dialed *Bhaiya* from his contact list and uttered, 'Bhaiya, I'm at UMass, Kanav rocked at the presentation. His CrushList rocks!' He hung up straightaway before his brother could respond. I wanted to hear his response. But he fulfilled his bet.

It was my turn. I spent the next five minutes doodling and gave him the desired result. He was astonished.

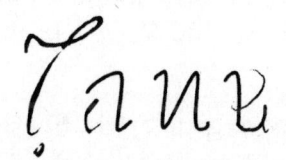

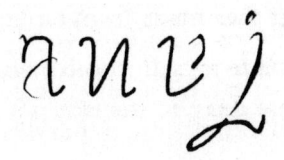

'Wow, you are quick!', he exclaimed.

An hour later, an SMS beeped on my cellphone. It was

Zaffer. I couldn't make it to the top 3 spots, having finished sixth. The judges said that my idea didn't give them an idea about how it'll make money. But still, they were eager to offer me incubation at a prominent start-up incubator. I'd to report there within five minutes.

Disappointed, I moved my drowsy body, leaving the computer with Anuj.

Two hours later, I returned after rejecting the incubation offer in US – stating the reason to be the fact that I wanted to start the venture in India and make it successful there, to change perceptions of NRIs that cool ideas don't work in India – as I intentionally crossed my eyes with Devyani all throughout, who was listening to me with rapt attention.

After the seminar, Dr. Devyani Padmanabham came up to me and said, 'Good show. All the best, I'm sure you would do well,' her words were my prize.

Victorious, I rushed back to the hostel to get to know about the whereabouts of Anuj's *bhabhi*. Anuj wasn't to be seen anywhere.

I found a sticky note on my window pane, which said. 'Sylvia was awesome. Now, I know why *bhabhi* left *bhaiya*.' I could barely smile.

I was jealous. At first I wanted to go to Sylvia. But she had finished fourth in the contest and I couldn't bear the sight of them ending up better than me – by investing the 'hard'-earned money that they made from tapes.

So, I made myself comfortable, instead I choose to write a note in my diary, to the lady who I'd forgotten all the while:

Tanya,
I'm feeling really bizarre. As a matter of fact, I am quite near to you. But sadly, I can't get in touch. Can't you take that promise away from me?

Can't you be a little less strict with a person you loved so much? I can wait for you, I have proven that. But, shouldn't this wait end soon?

You would have been proud to know that I finished sixth in the international business plan contest and they had offered my start-up an incubation here: but you know what, I didn't take that offer, as no matter how great this country is, I can't part away with India. Yes, I know you would be angry with me for not having enough motivation to be with you in this country, which might have become your second home by now, but I just can't force myself to like this country. You might have become used to this country, but India is what binds us together. Don't you think so? It is the place that brought us face to face with each other and it has helped me find my ambition, passion and love.

Sometimes, I feel as if you're never going to come back. I think what if you have already got committed to some American here. With the kind of wantonness that I have witnessed here in US, I feel all the more scared. But, I trust you. I know that when you can have the will power to stick to your principles and stay away from the person you love, you are not going to get affected by anything vile. Plus, this time I should really thank your monstrous family members for being there, guarding you from every 'bad things', including me.

I am feeling lonely in this lonely land, only wishing that you were around to accompany me as I go back to my land – our land. But I know that God is not kind enough to let my wish come true so soon.

Chapter 18:
THE FALL AT THE NIAGARA FALLS

My bags were packed. I was leaving UMass campus for Massachusetts, to see my mother and relatives. I was pretty excited about Niagara Falls, which my Mausi had planned for me over the weekend. Before I left for India, I had a week in hand to traverse the beauty of the wondrous country.

On my way back, I decided to see Sylvia off, after all she was my roommate and we had a pretty nice conversation in the beginning. I knocked their room. After a while, the door opened and Sylvia popped out her head and looked at me with furrowed eyebrows.

'Hey, may I come in?' I asked.

'For fight or for sex?' She asked sternly.

'For saying *au-revoir*. I am leaving, thought of saying goodbye,' I exercised my little French and managed to impress her.

I entered the room. Mark was sitting on the sofa, in just his trunks. I observed his well shaped body and an unforeseen fright shooed me from within.

What if both of them tie and beat me up mercilessly for what I'd done to them last day? Fortunately, things were in my favour.

'I came to say goodbye, Mark. I'm sorry for what happened.'

'*Merci.* We are sorry too. Au-revoir.' Mark said and stood up, and started walking towards me.

Sylvia came up to me and gave me a little hug, when I closed my eyes in gratitude. I was surprised when the hug was just about to get over, two kisses got implanted on both my cheeks. At the same time.

I opened my eyes, saw Sylvia and Mark snouts, pointing at me at less than ten centimeters from my lips and realized that I'd done a grave mistake in coming back to them. I gathered my luggage and rushed towards the door, on the way tumbling upon hitting a table.

'Hey, where are you going? Your good friend Anuj told us everything, about why you'd run away,' Sylvia yelled. Hearing Anuj's name halted my speeding footsteps.

'We understand that you are not *bi*, Cane-av,' Mark said to my relief and I sighed, only to hear later, 'but gay.'

With the velocity that I exited out of the hostel, it wouldn't be too much of an exaggeration if I say that I bet the speed of sound – in vacuum. Sorry for the nerdy joke.

My Mausi's place was nothing short of a palace. She wasn't my real Mausi, but my mother's school friend and she had migrated to US just after her marriage to Mausaji, who was the top tier executive at a prominent multi-national finance company. Mausaji remained so busy that most of the time, he was on tours and Mausi had learnt to be self-dependent. She was a very prolific blogger and was quite popular in the blogosphere, with her pen-name, *lady_lazarus*. She had even heard about my book but all the while, she never knew that I was her friend's son.

Mausi had two sons, both of whom were studying law at the State University, and were living in with their American girlfriends, for the past one year. Far from being traditional, Mausi instead championed live-in relationships: saying, 'kids become responsible by living in, it prepares them thoroughly for marriage.' Having already spent a week with my broad-minded Mausi, I could see drastic change in my mother's opinions and openness, when she said, 'Kanav, find a girl for yourself on your own. Don't expect us to find one for you.'

She had one scary German shepherd in house, who was interestingly called as Tiger, God knows why. When Tiger barked, it sounded like a roar and gave me nightmares in daytime. On the very first day, it walked up to me and started licking my shoes, when I kicked his neck in a reflex only to realize later that I committed a brave crime. It howled for 15 minutes straight and its every cry made my feet run colder and colder.

'Mausiji, please keep him tied,' I asked.

'Don't worry, he doesn't bite. Consider him like your younger brother,' she asked, fondling him with her long fingers.

I couldn't say anything. I desperately waited for the Niagara trip to quickly get over so that we could fly back to India. Being away from Tanya was less important than being away from Tiger. One good thing that had happened at my Mausi's place was that my mother had gifted all the *Amle-ka-murabbas* and *Chyawanprash* that she had carried for me to Mausi asserting that those were souvenirs for her from India.

Early Saturday morning, we packed our light backpacks and got seated in a comfortable Sedan. My Mom and Mausi in the front seat, while I, seated with my so-called younger brother, Tiger in the rear seat.

'What if it pees on the seat?' I asked, visibly concerned. Tiger looked at me, grunted, and moved his head towards the window, as if I was somebody much below his stature being offered a seat next to it.

'Haha, don't worry. He has been given the necessary toilet training,' Mausi said casually. I cringed in vexation.

Mausi was an amazing driver. Her pick-up speed was over 80s and she sped through the long multi-lane roads in minutes, straight into the expressways. After a long journey of around 9 hours, accompanied with sleep, coffee breaks at Starbucks, picturesque landscapes and occasional woofs by my younger brother, we entered the city with a funny name, Buffalo.

'Don't mistake this place to be Lalu Yadav's birthplace,' Mausi remarked, causing us to chuckle.

We had to stay at the motel for a day before witnessing the morning beauty. We arrived at a Holiday Inn, where there was a long queue of cars, waiting. Mausi swiftly parked the car outside and we went inside the Inn, along with Tiger.

The next morning was going to be spectacular. A few hours from Buffalo, resided the splendid beauty.

~

The morning sun got overshadowed by the mist in front of me. We were riding in the mist on a boat known as 'Maid of the Mist Boat Ride'. It took a long route to let us come face to face with the majestic fall. Niagara Falls. There were over fifty people on the boat, including an Indian family. We were engrossed, counting every passing second waiting to see the magnificent sight. The SLRs were geared up, safely hidden under our funny plastic suit to protect us from being drenched in the mist. Ten minutes of long wait and lo! Baffling, incredibly gorgeous and wondrous, the sight that beheld my eyes, made my eyes wet; my heart humbly saluted the Almighty for his unparalleled creativity.

There were howls, screams of joy and even cries hailing from all the corners of the boats upon seeing one of the most gorgeous natural sights of the world. I pulled out my camera, tried to snap a picture or two, only to realize later that I was shivering – in ecstasy. I sat back, kept staring without blinking, completely awed and speechless.

I just wished that Tanya was around. Her absence never made me feel as lonely as I was on that day. I was so lost that I didn't move for the next fifteen minutes, till we were right in front of the waterfall. I even forgot to click a picture of the rare beauty, when my mother, who had by now befriended an Indian family, tapped on my shoulders and reminded.

I wished to remain there, forever, with Tanya on my side. I wanted to paint it on canvas, though I had no idea how to even rightly hold a toothbrush, leave aside paint-brushes. My desire remained a desire and the boat crawled back to the harbour.

'*Beta*, say *namaste* to Mathur aunty. She lives in Massachusetts as well; they are here on a holiday.' My mother called me, to greet the Indian lady who Mausi and Mom had befriended. She had a very cute daughter, who was sitting on the seat on her husband's lap. Her husband looked very stern, much like a professor, and was taciturn enough to not indulge in the ongoing conversation.

I cursorily greeted her and began dabbling with my camera. I wasn't interested in meeting anyone, I just wished for Tanya. Meanwhile, my mother started recounting all my academic achievements to them, right from how I came 2nd in my 4th grade to how I cracked JEE. I was mortified. I felt like jumping out of the boat into the cold Colorado river and swim to Ontario, Canada.

The non-stop womanly banter stopped when we returned back to the Sedan. They invited us to their place in Massachusetts, on lunch the next day. The only good thing on the way was the wonderful ice-cream that I ate. A long drive later, we were back to where we began. Home.

I was so tired that I straightaway jumped into bed and fell asleep.

Chapter 19:
MRS. MATHUR, LULU AND …

'*Beta*, get up. We have to go to Mrs. Mathur's place.' My deep sleep was disturbed by a familiar voice. I got up, looked at my watch and cried, 'Damn, I thought it was afternoon. It is 8 am Mom, come on.'

'So what? Don't you have to take bath? You smell like your socks.'

'At least I was not aware of it in my sleep. Let me sleep for another one hour,' I said and dropped off.

Some time later, I felt as though some liquid was crawling over my bowel. I got up, perplexed and retracted from fear. It was Tiger, licking my navel out of every organ I possessed. It started barking, and my heart froze in fear. My Mausi came running by and instead of helping me out, she cheerfully caressed Tiger and said, 'Tiger! What baby, do you like playing with Kanav *bhaiya*?'

I can't express how much I hated the word *bhaiya* that early morning. Firstly it reminded me of Anuj's bhaiya and secondly, I was subtly being complimented as a dog. I wanted to run away, I wanted to be consumed by the wall I was leaning against; I wanted to kill all the pet dogs with the name Tiger in the world.

Thankfully, Mausi took it along with her. My sleep was

history and thanks to navel-molestation, I went to bath straightaway, a step that stumped my mother, who was sitting in the other room.

At noon, we left for Mrs. Mathur's place. It was half an hour ride from our place. At first, I didn't want to go but when my Mausi told me that this time, Tiger wasn't coming along, I eagerly joined them. Though I realized that it was going to be just a womanly get-together, with Mr. Mathur being at his office, but the lure of free Indian food was good enough to keep me motivated.

We arrived at her place and pressed the call bell. Mrs. Mathur came, greeted us followed by her cute child nicknamed Lulu, who was riding on her bicycle, which had supporting wheels. We sat down. She brought a plethora of appetizers to let us begin straightaway. There were so many items, that it could be foreseen that she had woken up very early and done all the preparation. She confirmed saying that they indeed were early risers. Then, my mother, Mausi and Mrs. Mathur indulged in womanly banter, leaving me cast out totally. I went to play with Lulu, who was in no mood to interact with me over her newly bought bicycle.

Suddenly, Mrs. Mathur came up to me and asked me to go to inner room and find out some books to read from the shelf. As I was about to enter the inner room she screamed, 'No, don't go into that room. The next room!'

I became confused. As directed, I entered the other room. There was a balcony and a huge library carrying a lot of management books, a sight which seemed horrendous because it reminded me of someone with the email id debashish_wharton@gmail.com. I carried so much hatred within me against the MBAs that I didn't want to read any books on management, no matter how many people were eager to move my cheese.

I instead went up to the balcony and began staring outside. There were a lot of tall Eucalyptus trees, with lush green grass, circumscribing the fence of their duplex. My spell was suddenly broken by the sound of a mild sob, coming from the window next to my balcony – from the adjacent room, the room that I was going to enter the first time. I peered across, the window had curtains which rendered it impossible for me to see anything.

I carefully listened, it was a womanly voice. The door of the next room creaked all of a sudden and somebody entered with a thud.

'For whatever reason you are crying, you need to stop it. Are you even listening to me? There are guests in our house and I need you to freshen up and greet them. Come on, wash your face. Don't make me come again. Wait, I have got a solution to fix your crying, there's a boy outside, from India. Come and talk to him,' it was Mrs. Mathur's voice.

I quickly retraced my steps and caught hold of a random self-help book, as I felt that Mrs. Mathur would be coming to my room. Indeed, she came and asked, '*Beta*, lunch is ready, rather than sitting and getting bored in our womanly talks, I would suggest you to meet my niece and interact with her. I would ask her to come here.'

I was utterly confused. Now that she couldn't handle her depressed niece, she was handing over the difficult task to me. Hell, no!

I grimaced and said, 'Niece?'

She said, 'Yes, she lives with us, is interning at MIT, this year, in Economics. Unfortunately, she had a presentation there and she couldn't accompany us to Niagara last day. She's as bright as you.'

'Is her name Tanu?' I asked, confused.

'How do you know that?' She asked, frightened. Her face became as though I had spoken something forbidden. I could not believe in coincidences. I was at Anuj's crush's place.

Wow! But why was she crying? And before that, what should I answer Mrs. Mathur?

'Oh…I found it written over … this book … I mean one of the books here,' I said fearfully.

'I wonder why would she not write her full name on a book', she replied in a doubtful tone, but left soon, saying, 'anyway, come and take your lunch', as my mother and Mausi had been left stranded by her for quite some time.

I dabbled with books for a while, when I heard Mrs. Mathur shout: 'Tanu, come here.' I was curious to find out how did Anuj's newest crush look like.

I went outside, turned to the right and there she was. *There she was. Tanya.*

My pupil had widened so much that I could see an aura behind her. She was gaping at me, as if she was yelling *what are you doing here?* to me. Five feet away, I could feel her heartbeats, she could see tears welling up in my eyes, I could not dare to blink; she could not dare to drift her eyes away. Her eyes didn't water, for she had already shed plenty a while ago. I smiled at her, a smile that took significant efforts on my end. She was wearing a blue t-shirt and a long skirt, her eyes had sunken in, dark circles surrounded those little beauties that once shone in ecstasy and her lips were as dry as a desert. I could never imagine that God was so wicked; he called me in the lion's den to meet a person, who I'd waited for forever.

'Hi, I'm..,' she said. The voice reverberated in my entire soul. I'd been missing to hear that very voice for God knows when.

'Tanu,' I immediately interrupted her, to make her nervous. She saw the face of Mrs. Mathur, who was eyeing at us, 'Aunty told me,' I said, relaxing her.

'I'm ahem ahem,' I coughed and muted my name, when suddenly, my mother called me at the peak of her voice, 'Kanav, *Beta* Tanu come and grab your plates.'

'Coming Mom,' I said, trying to conquer my tear clogged voice. I let go of my tears, pretended as though I was hit by a dust-storm and went to the washbasin.

'Let's go,' she said, as soon as I finished splashing water into my eyes. We gathered our plates, without saying a word.

'You know what Kanav, Tanu is doing an internship at MIT. Had you studied well, even you could have got an internship, but you – write worthless books and waste your life,' my mother chided me, causing Tanya to look at me, puzzled.

'I wish I had studied well, Mom,' I said, and stealthily winked at her.

We took our plates and went inside the room, away from the ladies talks, into the solace of my heart. I still had no idea whether she was still in love with me or not.

'Hi Tanu ji,' I said sarcastically, laying especial emphasis on her new name. She didn't reciprocate, got busy in eating the delicious delicacies. To quote a line from my first novel: 'when good food is placed in front of a girl, she forgets about everything else.'

'Now that I have unknowingly broken the promise of not talking to you, I think we can have a conversation,' I said. She didn't respond for a while. I thought that she was still not able to accept the fact that all this was a reality.

'See, without even letting you know I made it to your home,' I said in a conceited tone.

'Remember what happened the last time you entered my den?' She shot back. I let out a huge sigh.

'Thank God, your sarcasm still remains alive,' I said.

'It's used only for specific people,' she said.

'People you love,' I said.

'People I hate,' she retorted. For the first time she was staring at me, directly into the eyes. I didn't move my eyes and we played blink for over 2 minutes, without saying a word, when I lost to a sneeze.

'Wait a minute, you are talking to me. Why didn't you respond to my mail?'

'Which mail?'

'Oh my God,' I started laughing bizarrely, 'Oh my God, all the while I was thinking that you intentionally didn't reply to my mail. I had sent you a mail at *ilovebutterscotch@gmail.com*. You did not check it, right?'

'Yes, I don't login into that account anymore. I have changed my email id after coming back from India. I no more love butterscotch, you see,' she said, sarcastically.

'Who do you love then? You must have got a boyfriend around here, till now?' I asked, fearfully.

'Yes, he's American. Jason.'

'Wow. I thought so. I'm so happy for you,' I faked an excited voice.

'And yesterday, your friend, Anuj, escaped a slap from me,' Tanya changed the topic completely.

'Oh yes, what happened with him?' I anxiously questioned.

The previous day

Anuj was pretty confident that he would be able to charm Tanu and would be able to have a good time in the next one month that he was going to stay in US. He had already befriended one of Tanu's co-interns and got to know that she was single. He schemed a strategy to have an uncalled date fixed.

During the lunch break, he asked one of Tanu's friends to help him out with the proposal. She warned him that Tanya wasn't interested in having a relationship. But still, Anuj persisted and made her friend Sarah bring Tanya to Coffee Junction, during the lunch time. Anuj joined both of them portraying him as Sarah's friend and Sarah left in the middle, leaving both of them together, saying that she would be back in 15 minutes.

'So...' Anuj mumbled in front of Tanya.

'So?' Tanya bounced back.

'So, Tanu. What do you like?' Anuj began his mission impossible. His cheap tricks could have worked in case of random girls on facebook, but Tanya was way out of his league.

'I don't like such questions for sure,' she said, irritably. She was getting suffocated, in his clingy company.

'You know what, I am from IIT Delhi. Have you heard about it?' Anuj said. Having nothing less to talk about, he resorted to his favorite topic: IIT Delhi. Tanya was repulsed to the topic.

'I am seriously not interested in all of that.' Having faced her life's worst moment in and around IIT the last time she was around, she had no interest in all that jazz.

'Okay, you would be interested in this. I have started this really interesting startup called CrushList. It's the best way for people who are shy not to chicken out while exclaiming their love to their crushes,' Anuj said, trying hard to impress the pretty lady, taking the credits from me without thinking that I would ever get to know.

Indeed, Tanu got interested. She asked, 'Wow, that's interesting! How does it work?'

He explained the way and she got all the more interested and asked him a question, 'what was the inspiration behind starting all this?'

'I have a friend in IIT. His name is Kanav. He is such a bloody wimp that he just couldn't talk to girls. I thought why not I do something for such people and created the website,' Anuj explained pridefully, unconscious that he had just poured petrol over his own body and given Tanu the matchbox.

'Impressive. Did this Kanav friend of yours get a girlfriend?'

'Oh yes, he got a girlfriend. Tanya is her name. He proposed to her through my website only. The girl has moved to US now, though. He has moved on, I guess. He was dating a few chicks a while ago. Even I introduced him to one.'

'Wow, amazing. So much of social service, you are up to,' she said sarcastically. Anuj, unaware of Tanya's fluent sarcasm, mistook it as a compliment and even thanked her.

'I made something for you,' Anuj said.

'Really? What? Cake?' She asked.

'No, close your eyes and only then I will give,' Anuj said, expecting too much from Tanya.

'Come on, leave all that bullshit. Give it to me,' Tanya's bluntness crushed Anuj's expectation of creating a romantic ambience.

He, without much pomp and show, took out the ambigram and handed over to her. Holding the ambigram in her hand, she was taken aback.

'You have drawn this?' She asked Anuj, in a very strict tone.

'Yes. It's called as an ambigram. If you…' he began explaining.

'I know what an ambigram is. Stop blabbering,' she reprimanded him.

'Have you made this?' She asked again, in a more fierce tone.

'Yea…' Anuj stammered; his body language in complete incongruence with his voice.

'I am asking for the last time. Have you made this or Kanav?' She said in a very low voice. Anuj's pursuit for Tanu became history. He was flabbergasted by her clairvoyance.

How did she know that it was made by Kanav? He kept thinking. He had no idea about how to tackle the strictness of girls.

'I'm sorry I lied. I didn't know that you have read his novel. I also lied about CrushList. It's Kanav's venture. But, I didn't lie about him dating other chicks. He was dating, for sure. I'm sorry once again,' he let out a huge cry, surrendering himself completely to her. He was sweating profusely; it was the first time that a girl had dominated him completely.

'Where is Kanav? Where the hell is Kanav?' She yelled. Anuj didn't realize why she was yelling.

'He is in Massachusetts, perhaps at his aunt's place. Why?

Do you want to take his autograph?'

'Yes, that's what I wanted. Thank you,' she got up, walked away and asked just before she left, 'What's the title of his novel?'

'Oops! I fell in love!' Anuj replied, perplexed.

'Ha-ha! You shouldn't have ragged him like that. Poor fellow,' I said, after listening to the entire story from Tanya.

'He was a bloody liar. Why shouldn't I have? Anyway, so dating new chicks.'

'Yes. Dated five of them.'

'Just five.'

'Yes, settled on the five. Shivani Mishra. A child prodigy,' I said, confidently.

'Hmm,' she said trying hard to hide her dejection.

'How is Jason?' I asked.

'Who Jason?' She asked, being inattentive, lost in her thoughts.

'Your boyfriend,' I caught her lie red-handed.

'Ah, he's great. Six feet three inches tall, plays ice-hockey. When did you write a book?' She quickly drifted the topic.

'When I fell in love with Shivani. It was an enchanting experience. I remained sad for over 15 days when you'd left but thought that you were right. I didn't value respect. I realized that you didn't deserve me, you deserved someone better,' I said, trying my best to restrain my smile.

'What does she do?'

'Currently, she is doing a Ph.D. in Eastern Mythology, after finishing her three Masters.'

'Sounds like an old woman. What's her age?'

'She is our age. As I said she has been a child prodigy, finished her schooling when she was just 14.'

'Wow. Is she blind?'

'Why?' I said, stunned.

'How could she choose you?'

'Love is blind, my friend,' I said, winking. She carried her morose face, and for the first time, forgot to eat her food.

'Do you love her?' She questioned.

'Absolutely. It's my love that made me write a book on her.'

'When did you publish your book?'

I carefully calculated in my mind so that she doesn't smell any guile and told her, 'two months after you'd left.'

'Didn't you feel the need to tell me that you had got into a relationship?'

'No. You only asked me not to contact you ever,' I said, plainly, inwardly enjoying the ongoing tussle.

'So, you thought I would be okay with it?'

'Yes. You are, aren't you? You have your Jason, after all.'

'Yes. I do,' she whispered. Her voice was just on the verge of cracking. I thought I should change the topic.

'So Mrs. Mathur is your Mami? And that bald-headed clown-faced Mr. Mathur who I saw near Niagara is your Mama?'

'Yes, Paritosh. He is the one who knows that I'd an affair in India, my Mami doesn't know that. That's why she is a bit easy going. But, he's a mean-ass – being very strict,' she echoed my tone.

'Now you are placing disrespect over love for your family-mates,' I said, teasing her.

'You can disrespect when there is no love,' she replied, mildly. It struck a deep chord with me and I reflected upon our last meeting at IIT Delhi, when she left me all alone, helpless. I felt ashamed and remorse grabbed me, once again.

'I'm sorry for that day. You have no idea about how bad I felt all the while about what I said that day?'

'It's okay. It's good that you have moved on,' she said watching the ceiling, as though missing lizards on her wall, that reminisced of her days in India.

'So have you,' I said. She didn't respond. The dishes on my plate were finished and I needed to go out and take more, but I didn't feel moving even an inch, as my eyes had been glued to her eyes. There was an awkward pause when I decided to break it.

'So, Mami allowed me to sit along with you? As far as I remember, they were very strict.'

'Mami is strict, but to Divya, not to me. Mama keeps an eye, though. Over the last few months, they have become less strict, since last time when I returned back to US, my mother could see how much I despised you and asked Mama to let me loose, a bit.'

'That's how Jason came into being, right?'

'Oh…yes, right.'

'So, your Mama and Mami must be knowing about him and have no objections to it.'

'Oh yes…' was her natural response but she immediately corrected herself, and said, 'actually no. Mama is not cool. He is my Mom's brother, remember? However, Mami has become a little cool on me.'

'Hmmm. You are again hiding about your boyfriend from them – basically lying to them?'

'Yes,' she said in a hesitant tone.

'Anyway, you must be really happy now! A tall and handsome boyfriend, an internship at the MIT, an easy going guardian: what more does a person need to be happy?'

'True. I am absolutely happy,' she said, faking a smile. She avoided her eyes from me.

'And that's why you had been crying since yesterday, in your room?' I shot the arrow that I'd kept hidden for so long.

'What? Crying? Who?' She was stumped. She could not believe and started to move out, with her dish in her right hand.

'You,' I grabbed her left wrist from behind before she could flee outside. It was a magical and astounding touch after almost three months. She was frightened to turn back. She persisted, jerked her hand twice so that I would leave it, but I didn't.

She moaned, 'Kanav, please leave.'

'Not so easily. First face me.'

'I am begging you, Kanav. Don't torture me anymore,' she was already sobbing. Her voice resembled a frog, who had been kept away from water for long.

I went in front of her, she had lowered her face and was silently weeping. I took over the dish from her hand, kept that on the table, and lifted her face by her chin. We were inches away. I wiped her tears with my fingers, caressed her cheeks with my palms and stared right into her eyes. They had intense longing in them and they found solace in mine, which complemented them with intense wait. I held her face. I had rarely felt so close to her, every drop of her tears brought deep guilt within me of having sinned. One strand of her hair fell in front of her eyes and landed just between our eyes. I blew air on her face and displaced the disturbing strand from my sight. It was a divine union. Just the two of us, Kanav and Tanya.

We were wrapped in each other's arms for the next few minutes. Her hands tightly held me as she let all her trapped feelings out as tears rolling down her eyes, warm breaths coming out of her mouth, mild sobs knocking her throat and watery nose dripping on my shoulder. Her hands grabbed my t-shirt tightly, her long fingernails scratched my neck, while I just held her as tightly as I could – as though I was never going to leave her. It was one of such moments, where I felt intense, pure love, without being adulterated by any trace of lust.

I waited her to come back to normal, as I moved farther away from her. My eyes rested on hers, relieved. Tireless wait had just been drowned in the ocean of love and our feelings, that resided somewhere deep down our hearts, had been whirled to the top of our minds.

Her eyes called for me, cried out to me to take her along with me and I inched closer to her, so close that I could sense her warm breaths. She was motionless all the while, either perplexed or lost, in ecstasy. I grabbed her arms tightly, and even she reciprocated. I moved my lips very softly towards hers, which were dry and rough; they touched, played and fought with each other to get lost in each other. Just as I tried to dominate, she responded unexpectedly, by getting balled over and throwing me aside. I was stunned, as though thinking delightedly that she was going to assault me. But fantasies don't come true so easily.

'Don't even move a step. Go away,' she said in a typical American accent. I wanted to seal my lips against her once again, suppressing all her anger in the sea of love.

Didn't she want me anymore? Did she not feel that the distance between us zeroed a moment ago, the walls came crumbling down?

'Why?' I asked.

She cried, 'You cheat. You were going to cheat on your girlfriend. How could you?'

'You were cheating on Jason!'

'I don't have any boyfriend. Jason was my imagination. But you: you are a cheat. All the while, I was waiting for you to become a better person, you cheated on me with Shivani and now you are cheating on her with me. You are the worst person I know. How could you?' She shouted.

'You only gave me the permission to move on, and asked me not to contact you. You can't say that I cheated on you with Shivani, and what I do with Shivani is none of your business,' I asserted, trying to make her more vulnerable.

'I can't believe you'll use my ideologies against me. You are a cheater. You desperate prick! You just want to get laid, much like every perverted friend of yours, right? I was so right in feeling that you didn't love me. Earlier I said that you were my favorite mistake. I take back my words. You are my life's biggest mistake,' her sob started once again. A sob is what can make even the prettiest girls look ugly. I had to stop that. I didn't know how.

'Hey hey hey. Chill. You know what I think? I think that I can do with two girlfriends. Shivani is my girlfriend in India, and you in US. What's the problem in that? And, you have got better tits, while she has a better bum. I can't leave any of you, moreover when she happens to be a figment of my imagination,' I said, at first in a serious tone, which cracked in a felonious smile a moment later.

'*Kutte!* You liar,' she screamed, and threw a cushion on me, which I caught and threw back at her. A million dollar smile was back on her face.

I ran across the room and caught hold of her, embracing her tightly in my arms.

'Hey, Mami would come. Move,' she got worried.

'God's not so unkind, that even before we get together, he would separate us,' I said and pulled her closer to me.

'Why didn't you want to meet me?' I asked. My face was resting on her shoulders.

'Because I believed that I hated you. The day you last mailed me and broke my promise, I thought that you would not have changed, and remained a jerk, even after getting so much time to move on,' she said and made me realize that she indeed had read my mail.

'And what changed your opinion all of a sudden?'

'My opinion hasn't changed. I still think that you are a jerk, but yesterday, when Anuj, after his disastrous attempt at proposing me, related to me that you had started seeing girls and had moved on, I felt devastated.'

'That's why you'd been crying for the last one day.'

'Yes. I couldn't believe it. The person I had been waiting all the while to start valuing respect and claim me back had lost all respect from my eyes. I cursed my bad luck,' she said, now her cheeks filled with happy tears.

'By the way, how did you know that I was crying?' She asked, as she came out of her emotional self.

'Telepathy,' I winked to which she gave a *whatever* look. I took her near to the balcony, and continued, 'I eavesdropped from here, an hour ago.'

'You can hear from here?' She asked. We were standing apart.

'Yes, everything.'

'Let's go inside, else, if Mami goes into that room, she would burn all our romance.'

We went inside.

'Do you still hate me, for I broke your promise?'

'I hate you. But I realized that I love you more,' her eyes twinkled as she said those words.

She clenched my shirt, as if she would never let me leave her. All of a sudden, I turned back and grabbed her from her waist, and her torso collided with my body. I closed my eyes and felt her.

'I love…' I said, 'doors…' and threw Tanya off my hands in fear. She tumbled on the ground. I was nervous. The door had creaked, and it got open with Lulu on the other side, making me so nervous that I wanted to run to the balcony and jump out of the house.

Tanya, seeing the open door, quickly got to the other side of the room. We were no more inches, but six feet apart. Lulu cycled inside when Tanya screamed, '*Divya*, what are you doing here?'

'Isn't she called Lulu?' I asked Tanya.

'That's my nickname. Divya is my real name. *Bhaiya*, why did you throw Didi off your hands?' Divya asked, in a cute American accent. I was nonplussed. I looked at Tanya's face for a smart answer to which she looked absolutely shocked and clueless. My mind started racing.

'We were fixing the curtains Lulu, but unfortunately your Didi is too heavy for me to lift,' I fabricated an exaggerated lie out of thin air. Both Tanya and me let out a silent sigh.

She laughed. Tanya called Lulu and whispered to her, 'Don't tell your Momma about it. She would again rub green chillies in your teeth. I'll bring you chocolates in the evening.'

Lulu got frightened, unaware about her elder sister's trickery, and finally said, 'Okay. I will never tell. And Tanu, Momma was calling you and *bhaiya*, for ice-cream.'

'Is butterscotch there?' I asked Lulu. She affirmed. I winked at Tanya.

'We are coming, in 2 minutes, have to finish our food. You go ahead,' Tanya instructed Lulu. She pedaled out on her mini bicycle.

We immediately finished our unfinished task, as we locked the door. Against the door, against the walls, against the floor. Two minutes of delightful tussle. It was the dessert for us.

'I miss butterscotch. I am falling in love with it all over again,' Tanya said, with her wildly disheveled hair.

'Don't you miss my braces?' I said. She froze in the gruesome memory.

We rushed outside. We went to the dining table, sat on diametrically opposite ends with butterscotch ice-creams, when Mrs. Mathur asked us, 'So, did you guys have fun?' I analyzed her question to have any sarcastic tinge, but thankfully, there was none. I quickly replied, 'Yes, we had awesome food. Especially the dessert.'

'Great!' Mrs. Mathur exclaimed.

'*Beta*, do eat *amle ka murrabbas*. It's good for the mind,' my mother said, 'Your Mami knows how to make it.' My mother started her favorite topic, this time to Tanya. She appreciated my mother's concern, and affirmed. I interrupted my mother, 'Ma, she's already pursuing an internship at MIT, do you need anything more?'

'Wow, just an hour of friendship, and you have already shifted sides. I fear what would happen to me when you bring your wife?' My Ma taunted, making everyone laugh.

'Oh Ma, don't start in front of everyone,' I whined.

After ten minutes, we left. I kept staring at Tanya from the rear view mirror until she disappeared from my view. She had given me her number, but said that she liked it when we didn't talk. Now being inspired from me, she wanted to write a novel outlining her experience, but before that she wanted to read my book, the e-book of which I'd to mail her as soon as I got back.

She gave me a chit and asked me to open when her sight faded from the car. I opened it. It was a page from her diary. Something was scribbled on it. I read on.

It was the happiest day of my life. Thanks for being my favorite mistake. And the best part is: I loved your Mom; she's so funny, unlike you.

Let's carry on with our pledge of not speaking with each other, and just writing to each other until I come back to India, since I realize that it has actually fostered our creativity. I have been writing a poem a day ever since I left you and all I could present you today for giving me the wonderful surprise of today is one of those poems.

The Slap of Loneliness

The loneliness slaps you on the face
Tells you that you'd been wrong
You faced so much turmoil,
For someone, who is not going to be along

You fight it, hoping to win
Losing the battle, with every passing moment
You strive, this time
Hoping not to lose, this time again
It pays in the end,
When you come out of the ordeal
You have become strong, tough
And the world looks more real

Then you find him
He tells that he never left you
Rather, you'd left him
When you left yourself, true?

'So, you liked Tanu a lot, it seems?' My mother woke me up from my contemplative stance. I was dumbfounded. *What was she up to?*

'Come on Mom,' I muttered, in irritation.

Three days later, after carefully assigning the window seat to my mother and letting her enjoy the full journey back home without any disturbance, I returned back to Delhi. Prof. Virgo didn't dare to come to receive me, that time. I spent the rest of the time at home, eating heinous yet healthy food like *karele ka juice, amle ka sharbat* and other such disgusting items, counting my days to come back to Delhi. I had just two tasks: working on my crush and CrushList.

Chapter 20:
LIGHT CANDLES, NOT CIGARETTES

Early July

The holidays were over. I had just arrived at the hostel, delighted after having an almost successful vacation. As soon as the guard saw me, he instructed me to rush to the badminton court. When I asked why, he didn't say a word and made a straight face at me. Something seemed to be wrong. Terribly wrong!

The morbid smell proved the same. I rushed to the court. The entire batch was there, surrounding something. It was the first time that I arrived in the hostel to be greeted with blank hapless faces rather than smiling ones. I searched through the faces to locate Aryan, Sameer or Anuj. They were standing on the side, with their morose faces, perhaps for the first time in their lives. I rushed to the center to find out what was so ominous that had taken away every sign of happiness from the faces of all my batchmates.

As I made my way to the forefront through the abominable lull, wrestling my shoulders against the crowd, I felt my feet getting stiffened. I didn't want to move ahead as I realized what I was to behold one step ahead of the crowd. Just when I was about to stop, I felt a comforting hand on my shoulder as it escorted me to the front. Aryan.

'Be strong,' Aryan said.

There was a body wrapped in white lying on the ground, surrounded by a stark silence that was only broken by the mild sobs of my batchmates Sarthak and Kshitij. The face of the corpse was covered. Everyone's eyes were wet and I stood there, stupefied. Never before in my life had I been so scared. I didn't want to think about who it would be inside that white sheet. I wanted to run back to my home, to never come again, to never know who I was never going to see again. Alas, I couldn't stop my mind to wander.

I could not utter a word. Horrified, I looked at the faces. Every face of my batch was present, except one that lay beneath that white sheet. I encountered a tornado in my heart when I realized that it was the person who always met me with a smile that held his cigarette. Manas.

'Manas,' I shrieked and burst into tears. I got so frightened that my feet started shuddering. Aryan held my shoulders and escorted me to the other side where Anuj and Sameer were standing.

'How did it happen?' I stuttered. Seeing his corpse in the hostel, I suspected a suicide but could not convince myself of the fact that a person as jolly as Manas could do it.

'He puked blood the entire last night and didn't even tell us about it. When Sarthak, his roommate, found that out he urged to rush him to the hospital. But, he didn't comply saying that he doesn't want his mother to know that he smokes and he would get better. We adhered to his wish until this morning, when he lost his senses. When he was taken to the hospital, he had suffered severe blood loss, and doctors couldn't save him.'

'Why was he puking?' I questioned.

'The doctor said that one of his lungs had stopped functioning and his wind-pipe had been eroded over time, for almost two months now. He didn't tell anyone. He must have been barfing blood for two months, without letting anyone of us know,' Aryan explained.

'Because of smoking?'

The trio nodded. I could not believe what I heard. I looked at the dead body of a person – whom I had never heard saying anything bad about anyone, unlike all the other judgmental IITians like me that I'd encountered. He was always lost in his own world: contented in the smell, smoke and taste of his one and only love. *Marlboro.*

'Lately he had started smoking 30-40 strong Marlboro daily, besides rolling plain tobacco often,' Aryan said, 'and you know, this asshole – Anuj – is following his example with 20 per day.' Dumbstruck, I gave a how-the-hell-could-you-do-that look at Anuj.

'Not anymore,' Anuj uttered, relieving each one of us, and then started crying, like a baby. 'I hate myself. I hate myself,' Anuj uttered as he tumbled on to the ground. The entire assembly of my batchmates turned towards him in surprise.

'What happened?' Sameer asked in a broken voice, concerned. It was the first statement by him so far. I had never seen him so quiet before. His eyes were still inundated, so was everyone's.

'I am responsible for his death. I killed him,' he cried out loud. The ghoulish lull was ruptured by his shrill outcry and furrowed eyebrows had now taken over the blank faces.

'What? What are you saying?' Sarthak, who was also sobbing, yelled.

'I initiated him into smoking. I had a severe break-up and I started smoking, when he visited my room and I gave him a puff. Thereafter, we always used to smoke together. We used to buy packs alternately to smoke together. Then, I moved on with my next relationship which reduced my consumption, while he continued.'

'You had a break-up but Manas had no reasons to start smoking; he always looked happy, I had never seen him without a smile,' I spoke my mind.

'Smiles are just a way to hide one's sadness, brother. He had faced more tragedy than anyone else here, which is his personal matter that is not to be discussed here in public,' Aryan said.

'How do you know?' I asked Aryan, personally.

'He shared over a drink,' he said. I didn't have the courage to question further, though my curiosity didn't allow me to be still.

'Did you inform Manas' parents?' I asked the crowd.

'I had informed his Mom and asked her to come along with his Dad urgently, without telling her about the mishap. However, aunty asked me to separately inform his Dad. When I cut the phone, I couldn't find the phone number of his Dad in his cellphone, I didn't know what to do. Her Mom lives in Jhansi and would be arriving here in another five hours.' Sarthak said.

'What's the matter with his parents?' I sneaked away from the group and asked Aryan.

'Bro, he wouldn't have liked me telling it.'

'I understand.' I said, admiring Aryan's ethics, and walked away towards the group, only to hear Anuj losing his mind.

'I am a murderer. Had I not given him that first puff, we wouldn't be encountering this horrid day,' Anuj wailed and started hitting his head against the floor in desperation. We were getting annoyed.

'Stop it Anuj. You are not responsible. Stop doing that to yourself. Will you?' Aryan screamed and all of us turned mum, as he continued, 'while Manas was writing his JEE, his Dad was busy filing a divorce suit against his Mom. All throughout his preparations, his Dad was never at home. *Never at home,*' Aryan said, blurting out the secret that was perhaps the cause why Manas was stuck with his habit. But, it was only to curb something more disastrous that could have happened with Anuj.

'You are not responsible. Get your acts together. And, I'm sorry guys, I shouldn't have said,' Aryan said in a voice that was full of remorse, and moved out of the scene.

Anuj was flabbergasted. His wail had stopped. Despite being smoking buddies, Manas didn't share his sorrows with him. Sarthak got the answer why Manas' phone didn't have his father's number. And we got the reason to not talk for the next few hours.

I looked at the white sheet once again; the person who was no more was a person who truly knew how to live. He knew how to spread happiness without letting the world know of his sorrows. His strength to live encountered just one weakness: smoking and it had turned upside down. I recalled his happy face when after hearing Sameer's tragic tale during my birthday, he wished me good night, with his cigarette. No matter how many memories of his came into my mind, there was a cigarette in each of them.

I looked at Sameer. He was the quietest person around. He didn't speak much for the next three days either. Minutes later, our hostel warden came and the body was taken to the IIT hospital and we were asked not to follow, as Manas' mother would be coming. I couldn't even dare to think what would happen when she would have found out that the only person who was there in her life, had given up to smoking.

Manas' death had an innate transformation in each one of us. We started valuing our lives, our reasons of joy and sorrows more and most importantly: all the five chain smokers of my batch gave up smoking. Manas managed to induce his goodness in our lives even after he had gone away.

※

A month later, five of us friends, drove to Jhansi to meet Manas' mother. It was the least we could do for a friend who had left an unfilled hole in our lives. When we pressed the door bell, a man opened the door. We introduced ourselves as Manas' friends and he invited us in, called Aunty by her name and he completely surprised us when he introduced himself as Manas' Dad. Amidst irreparable sorrow, Manas even managed to bring in one tinge of joy at his home by bringing his parents together.

As we watched through the childhood pics of happy Manas with his beautiful mother and handsome father, aunty came in and upon seeing us, she mildly greeted. Her disheveled hair, dark circles and the vacuous look on her face clearly showed the turmoil that she had gone through and was still going through. We handed her some of the pictures of Manas that we had snapped during birthday parties, outings and get-togethers at the campus.

She started crying, upon seeing one snap where he was smoking. We realized that it had been a faux pas on our end not to have filtered the pics. But it was too late for a realization. Her face turned red in rage and she yelled in an outburst, 'why on Earth did he have to smoke? If he had been around, I would have ruthlessly beaten him.'

It hit us hard and we could sense the agony a mother undergoes upon finding one bad habit that her ideal child imbibes from bad company. The company of us.

'Do you guys also smoke?' Aunty asked in a broken voice.

Only Anuj, amongst the five of us who were there, used to do it but he did it no more. We sensed that Anuj was prompted to say something - something remorseful about him initiating Manas into smoking and very tactfully, Aryan took charge and said, 'None of us, aunty. It's very unfortunate that Manas got this habit. We are glad to inform you that all the smokers of our hostel have left smoking forever, after what had happened.'

'After they saw my son dying out of it. That's so unfair, isn't it? Why does it take someone to die to make people understand that smoking is bad? Tell me, tell me, Aryan. Why can't they understand on their own and stop it?'

We had no answer. Her emotions, her anger, her agony were completely justified. We just looked down in guilt. *Why does it take someone to die to make people understand that smoking is bad?*

Uncle escorted her inside and told us that she was still not over the depression. To take their minds off the mishap, Uncle along with Aunty had started campaigning for anti-smoking actively in Jhansi and nearby areas, where they organized rallies and awareness camps in college-campuses. After handing him some of Manas' books and notebooks, we bid them our silent goodbyes and departed.

We returned, almost all of us in contemplation, as none

of us spoke a word during the first two hours of the return journey.

'Let's invite Uncle and Aunty to IIT for an anti-smoking rally,' Anuj broke the lull.

'Great idea,' we reciprocated.

'When?' Aryan questioned.

'As soon as possible. I'll arrange everything. Permissions, mics, candles,' Anuj said, 'Kanav, you start publicizing it on the social media. We'll make it grand.'

A month later, the rally did take place. I came up with different slogans for the cause to provoke people: 'light candles, not cigarettes', 'don't smoke, you'll suck bigtime', 'first smoke goes up, then the smoker'.

Around five hundred people turned up as we walked from the IIT main gate to Siri Fort carrying lighted candles. Aunty led the procession, accompanied by Uncle who carried Manas' portrait in his hands, and it was the first time in the last two months, or maybe in years, that there was a smile on her face. If there would have been one person happier than us to see her smile, it would have been Manas, whom we missed terribly on that day.

However, Manas didn't have to wait for long. Exactly one month later, Manas came alive, when aunty registered the NGO: *Manas Foundation,* to rehabilitate smoking addicts and campaign for the cause of anti-smoking.

Chapter 21:
THE PERFECT WOMAN

It took us a month after the day that took Manas away from us to get used to our regular college life. It was only in mid August, when things could actually become normal, after we met Manas' parents once more. We were happy to realize that aunty had gotten much better and kept herself busy with the work of the NGO.

After a long time, there was a smile of relief and satisfaction on our faces. It was during that time, that Sameer had started doing stand-up comedy to let go of our gloom and take our minds off our lost friend. With days, we actually started seeing him evolve as a humorist and we recommended him to the audition of a stand-up comedy gig, held at one of the prominent lounge of the city, Route 41 in Saket.

It was evening of late August, when I had just fixed a bug in my website that Sameer knocked on my door. 'Hey, thank you so much brother. They had selected me for the stand-up gig of this Friday. The theme is women, and you are the first person I'm telling it to.'

'Congratulations buddy. I'm glad to see you here, and must say that I'm proud of you. I am extremely flattered to know that I'm the first person with whom you are sharing the good news,'

I said, wondering why I was chosen by him, when actually it was Aryan who suggested him to try for one. A minute later I got the answer.

'You know what?' He was overexcited as he began, 'it has been my long cherished dream. Thank you so much God,' he screamed at the ceiling – which had no trace of God, until and unless the dirty black lizard contained one.

'I need you to write something funny for me, please please please,' he knelt in front of me and begged with his folded hands. It was a funny sight. It tickled me so much that I chose not to respond for a minute.

I stood still like a statue, while he kept begging me like Kung fu Panda in deep meditation.

'Delegating a work straightaway? I am not glad to see you anymore,' I remarked haughtily.

'Please,' he cried like a baby. My stone heart melted.

'Okay, I will. What do you want me to write on?'

'The Enigma of the Perfect Woman. A guide for men to find the perfect woman.'

'Buddy, you are asking the wrong person I guess,' I said, after recounting my experience of the myriad unsuccessful dates that I'd once been a part of.

'See, I'm fat. It hurts me while I sit and plead. Don't make me do that once more. Please.'

'Okay I won't. But when I complete, you'll do that once for me.'

'Sure.'

We sat, outlined and summed together points to make it an interesting read. And then it took me fifteen minutes to give it a structure. Sameer read through:

"Google about how to find perfect guys. You'll find numerous articles saying who to date and who not. But hardly there will be articles which could tell you what kind of girl you should date.

"I take it upon myself as my responsibility to enlighten the world about what kind of girls, if they actually existed, would have been perfect for guys. The Perfect Woman. The mystery unknown. The ultimate piece of Godliness. Here they come:

- **Date a girl who is well-read:** *Yes, friends. Being well-read is important. Being well read doesn't mean having read all Bhagat's books. Not even Kanav's books (see, I'm modest enough to take a dig at myself!). It means having a rich taste of good books. It assures you that the girl has a taste, a preference, that she won't take shit. And if she agrees to date you, it means you're something. How's that for confidence? This also assures that she would prefer 'hi' to a 'hieeeee' whenever you meet her.*

- **Date a girl who is funny:** *Almost sixty percent of the girls when asked what is the one quality that they would want in their dream-man, say 'sense of humour' or 'someone who would make me laugh'. While they easily pass on the difficult baton to us, since humour is, by no means, an ordinary talent; they forget to realize that even a man could desire some fun. Now don't twist your head, I'm not talking that kind of fun. In this multitude of sentimentality, it's a rarity to find a 'sense of humour' in the fairer sex, however keep your eyes open. Some woman with the fragrance of nitrous oxide might pass by. That's laughing gas, dumbass! (pardon my pathetic sense of humour!)*

- **Date a girl who is not-so-gorgeous:** *While most of us desire, and at some level, even fantasize about dating gorgeous girls, but let me tell you, almost 99% of them are very fussy. They'll make your life hell. Trust my experience. A not-so-gorgeous girl is perfect. She would listen to you, treat you like a teddy bear rather than a pet dog and you* *could make even your friends with gorgeous-girlfriends jealous by letting them know how teddy-bearish you feel like.*

- **Date a girl who has an ambition:** *Now this may sound preachy but it pays in the long run. The woman must have something other than you, gossiping and shopping to keep her busy with. It might be a desire to become a paragon in cooking, teaching, business or writing misandrist blogs. Or even changing the country. Ambition. It's a prerequisite, gives you breathing space and keeps her happy without extra effort on your part. Also, in case you happen to be a total sucker, this would run your home!*

- **Date a girl who is cool:** *This is very important. They should be cool with everything except three or more some. Yes, if she gets over-protective or over-concerned for you, just tell her to get lost since you already have your Mom for such cute things. How would you ascertain on your first date that she's cool? Well, this is a tough nut to crack. But I've a trick. Tell her that you don't like her and check her reaction. If she is cool, she would remain cool. And if she's not, then make sure you know the nearest hospital around.*

- **Date a girl who likes you, rather than admires you:** *Liking doesn't require a reason. Admiration does. Admiration creates walls, makes you larger than life. Liking breaks walls, makes the liker likable. Admiration is for your qualities, liking is for you. I'm assuming that you're not a total loser. Pardon me if I erred. Did you like this piece of advice? Now you can like my facebook page!*

- **Once, for few days, date a girl who is rich and spoilt:** *This is guy's side of the story. There is no such thing as free lunch for only those who haven't seen this side of the world. Always manage to date at least one rich girl, with a big car and a Louis Vuitton purse, so that later you could tell your grandson that you were nothing less than a Superman when you were young. Tell your chunnu-munnus about how you once dated a hot chick, who had a Beetle and who smoked pot, and dumped her when you got bored of her concern about the greenery in her* *purse rather than redness of your cheeks; and married their Dadi. If you are not a celeb like me right now, just follow this advice, you'll have a young fan following in your old age. Just make sure that the Dadi that you find for your grandchildren was more spoilt than the Beetle wali, else your Superman chaddi would be pulled down.*

- **Date a girl who is not too senti-menti:** *It's a heartbreaking statement but yes, a hefty percentage of girls are sentimental crybabies. If you're a girl and you get offended by this, you clearly know what I mean. Such girls spend the majority of their time drooling over some random crush of theirs, who might be already committed; getting fascinated by some random celebrity so much that even dreams are 'haunted' by them; getting all emotional about some random crap that some lunatic guy said about their weight or dressing style and in worst cases, for not being able to share bitchy stories about their acquaintances to their friends. Date a girl who's opposite of all these, who sheds tears only when she cuts onions and you cook!*

- **Date a girl who's got some talent:** *Talents are interesting. Encourage her to pursue them. Make sure that she never ever gives them up because of any reason whatsoever. Appreciate her. It'll make her happy with herself and in turn, make you happy, because your nights would be awesome. And nothing is greater than happiness. Thank you. Now you can clap.*

Sameer started crying in joy, and kept screaming, 'Thank you thank you,' for two minutes. It was the first step towards his dream-job of becoming a well-known public speaker. I felt happy that I could be of some use to him and I let him go off without making him become the Kung-fu Panda once again.

✾

Online talks had started between Tanya and me. The slapstick replies, whacky conversations, sarcasm wars were back into my life. Though things had been delayed from my end, as the shock of losing Manas didn't allow me to come to my normal self for a long time, but as it's said time heals wounds.

After August, things had become more or less stable. Our talks – online – went on for the next one year, as both of us got busy in our studies as well as our daily chores – which involved writing stand-up gigs for Sameer and managing *CrushList.in*, on my end and of topping her class (yes, she outshined every son-of-a-bitch there) and flirting with cute Americans at Tanya's end.

Thanks to *skype*, we never needed a cellphone number and ISD calls. We spent lesser than my batchmates who had girlfriends locally in Delhi. Moreover as she had got her own laptop in her third year, accessing internet was no more a taboo for her, as things got a bit lenient as she had adapted into the environment that had once appeared to be a cage to her. Ever since she had excelled in her studies, even Paritosh Mama had become very casual on her and no more spied on what she was up to. That was the ideology for every Indian home: if studies are on the right track, there is no need to worry.

It took me a lot of time to actually come out to my normal self and when I did, it was absolute fun. Often I used to drop messages on Tanya's email id, which she would reply as sarcastically as she could when she got time. And conversations continued.

Much like my previous book, many readers wanted more such conversations, so I compiled them once again, for all of you: The conversations are spread over the period of late 2009 to late 2010. Yes, one year passed by without any spectacular change in our lives. She was single, I was taken, and we were committed!

#1. Where I irritated her to the best of my ability

Tanya: I was totally nuts to have said a yes to you.
Kanav: Why? What's wrong with me?
Tanya: You are boring and irritating!
Kanav: So are you going to leave me? *expectantly*
Tanya: Yes.
Kanav: Thank you. B-bye.
Tanya: Once again, I was totally nuts to have said a yes to you. Huh, jerk!

#2. Where I outwitted her

Tanya: I read this wonderful line today: "When you are in love you can't fall asleep because reality is better than your dreams."
Kanav: I disagree.
Tanya: Really? May I know why?
Kanav: Because my truest love is sleep.
Tanya: Jerk!

#3. Where she killed my pomp in one go.

Kanav: I bathe daily even in this winter.
Tanya: So sad.
Kanav: Why sad, it's something that I'm proud of.
Tanya: Even then your dirty mind couldn't get cleaned.

#4. Where she bet my lover ego into pulp.

Kanav: Let's bring a change in your lives. Let's stop voice-talking on internet.
Tanya: Okay.
Kanav: How can you be so cool and say okay? Won't you miss me?
Tanya: No. Rather I'm glad that I would be saving power by not playing recorded 'hmms' in reply to your boring monologues.

#5. Where she pushed me at my wit's end & smashed.

Tanya: Describe me in one word.
Kanav: Mine.
Tanya: Aww, that was so cute.
Kanav: I meant coal-mine: courtesy your kajal.
Tanya: And I meant - *kutte!*

#6. Where I used her against herself. I'm smart! :D

Tanya: What gift do you want on your birthday?
Kanav: You.
Tanya: Me? That's sweet.
Kanav: Now that you are touched, get me an iPad. *wink*

#7. Where she appreciates my singing. Really?

Kanav(singing): Tu jahan jahan chalega, mera saaya saath hoga. (stops) (A minute silence, I expect applause. But there is no response from Tanya's side)
Kanav: How was it?
Tanya: Very soothing.
Kanav: Thanks. That's the first time someone appreciated my singing.
Tanya: I was talking about the silence, dumbass!

#8. When she read my first book.

Tanya: I read your book.
Kanav: So, what do you say?
Tanya: I liked it, especially the end.
Kanav: Yeah, it has a sad end. I knew sad ends are most impactful.
Tanya: No, dumbass. It's a happy ending. The girl gets free from the jerk, phew!

#9. When she tried to act smart and failed.

Kanav: What does your Mom think about me?

Tanya(smiling): She thinks you to be a wicked rascal and a repugnant prick.

Kanav(emotional): Would you do me a favour?

Tanya(concerned): Sure. Did you feel bad?

Kanav: A little bit, for her spoilt daughter, for she's been dating this wicked rascal and repugnant prick since the last one year. Now, did you feel bad?

Tanya: Wicked rascal!

#10. When she absolutely won my heart with her wit. I bowed down in front of her.

Kanav: Many a times, I think how could such a pretty girl like you fall for me?

Tanya(contemplative): Because we're so similar

Kanav(puzzled): How can you say that?

Tanya: Because many a times we think exactly the same thing!

#11. When she never let my head become too heavy for my shoulders

Kanav: One day, you'll be proud to know me.

Tanya: I just hope that when that day comes, you know me.

The conversations are never ending and they have prompted me to start a newspaper column, after I'm done with the release of this book. *How does that sound?*

Chapter 22:
AS TIME MOVED ON

Time passed by like an aeroplane goes out of the sight in the sky. From the recently joined *fachcha* of IIT, I was suddenly one amongst the senior most people of my college. The effect of time was not only mental but also physical as some portion of my hair went gray.

Tanya didn't come to India during this entire duration. She had gotten pretty much into her academics as she had to please her Mom and come back to India as soon as possible, since her mother had not been keeping well. Since she had already finished her first year in India with scintillating marks, she was promoted to the second year right as and when she had joined. By early 2010, she was in the final semester.

In her college, placements started in the summer time, unlike in IIT Delhi where it started in December and by the end of June, she had been shortlisted by major finance and consulting companies. The only feather on my cap during the previous one and a half years had been that my second novel *Ouch! That 'Hearts'..* was published, where Arpa, one of my prized readers came up with that catchy title. My start-up, *CrushList.in* was working okay – not too great, because I was unable to find out a proper business model other than advertisement for the same, which significantly lowered my enthusiasm to pursue it full-time, unlike what I'd earlier thought. Even I started preparing for jobs.

Coming back to Tanya, as you know, pretty girls need and rightly deserve attention much more than ugly boys like me. So it was June. Tanya wanted to join a company which had branches in Delhi NCR so that she could shift to India to spend time with her mother. As her day of interview came nearer, pressure built in my stomach. As she had told me, it was really difficult to convince the companies which are headquartered in US to allot the India offices as the HR division, responsible for hiring employees, of those branches would be in India.

Finally the day of her interview came. I spent that entire day getting worried and for the first time, I went to a Lord Hanuman temple just outside the IIT Gate and devoted *laddus* to him asking him to bring Tanya back.

It was the first time God had listened to me. Tanya had accepted an offer from McKonjee, a major strategy consulting company and as she had wished, they had offered her a position of a Business Analyst in Delhi with a whooping package of Rs.12 lacs per annum. I was happy as well as jealous. I was shown the real face of Delhi when I realized that much like government employees, even God worked efficiently on bribes.

It was one of the most satisfying moments of my life. Knowing that the person, who stayed away from you for around 3 years would be coming back, to be with you – for eternity – until you recalled that the villain was still to be tackled, and it again called for yet another box of *laddus* to Lord Hanuman to help you out.

Tanya's admission to McKonjee inspired me to prepare for the same company. How wonderful would it be for us to spend half the day together, without ever raising her mother's eyebrows? Plus, I had also heard that they send people together on foreign assignments – so I couldn't afford to miss the chances of getting fully sponsored honeymoons.

It was August 28th, 2010, 1 day prior to my birthday. Tanya had not talked to me for a couple of days; I could easily sense that she was planning a surprise. 1 hour before my birthday, as I was busy being idle in my hostel room, my cellphone buzzed.

I was surprised, as generally you don't expect someone to call you an hour before your birthday. It was my mother.

'Hello Ma, it's not 12 yet. Thank you yet again,' I joked to my Mom.

'Kanav,' my mother said, in a very serious tone.

'What happened?'

'Mrs. Mathur called. Tanu's mother is severely sick. Her neighbour had called them in US to arrange help for them here in Delhi.'

'What? Oh my God. Where is she now?'

'At her home. Her neighbours had called an ambulance. Rush to her as soon as possible. They don't have anyone else in Delhi other than their neighbours.'

'I'm on my way Mom, you don't worry.'

'Note the address,' she said.

'I know it. Bye,' I said, and disconnected, not realizing that I'd given my mother the evident hint about what was going on in my life.

I had no idea how to reach the other part of Delhi at 11 o' clock. Much like every other time, I went in search for Aryan

– the most resourceful guy in the campus, but he was nowhere to be found. Nobody even bothered to assist me as they were planning a surprise birthday bang for me, that was to include thousand ruthless bumps. After encountering listless non-answering faces for five minutes, I called Aryan. At first he didn't pick up. I called again. This time he picked up.

'Bro, need to go to Tanya's place immediately.'

'You can't get away without bumps, hero, no matter whether it is your girlfriend or family.'

'Bro, it's urgent. Tanya's mom is in a critical condition,' I panicked. I was worried for her and for Tanya. All my earlier hatred was dissolved in one go.

'What? Are you kidding me? I don't even have a car here right now.'

'Bro, run! Arrange a bike somehow. We need to rush.'

It didn't take him more than a minute to reach me with the key of Bajaj Pulsar of the senior: the same bike that played the role of a supporting artist in my second book. We flee like a hawk, at the speed that I had never experienced before. I was least bothered about the speed. Instead, the concern for someone's life was eating me alive. After encountering the demise of my friend Manas, I truly understood the value of life.

We crashed down the gate of Tanya's home, the bike halted after a long screech. The door was locked. Incidentally, the screech brought out a few neighbours and they told us that she had a severe heart attack and was rushed to Escorts. We rushed to Escorts, before they could ask who we were.

It was yet another high speed race with trucks for Aryan. On the route, my cellphone started buzzing. Never before had attention irritated me. I didn't pick up. I couldn't switch off my cellphone as my mother might have called to inquire about Tanu's mom. So all through the way, I kept silencing the calls.

A call with the US country code flashed into my screen and I picked it up, thinking it to be either Mrs. Mathur or Tanya inquiring about her mother. It was Tanya. I composed myself and said a fake excited *hi*. She shot several "muahhs" on phone and said that she had written a poem for me. I was baffled. I realized that Mrs. Mathur had wisely not informed her about the mishap. Hearing the noise of trucks in the background, she got a bit perplexed, and asked me where I was headed to. I lied that I was on way to India Gate, to celebrate my birthday there. I didn't tell her anything, as she told me her poem.

> *You fought all odds for me*
> *And see, today we won.*
>
> *When dark clouds hid the horizon*
> *You were my silver lining*
> *When I stumbled, you held me*
> *When I blundered, you forgave*
> *Not only had you put breath in my body*
> *You gave light to my soul*
> *Made me everything I am.*
> *Many times I've thought of thanking you*
> *But then I stopped myself*
> *Because gratitude is not enough*
> *Love is what is called for.*
>
> *On your birthday, Kanav*
> *I just want to say*
> *That I'm proud to have you in my life*

I had just reached Escorts when she finished her poem. I started crying like a baby. She thought I became emotional on her poem, which was indeed very touching. I wanted to hug her and tell her that her Mom(aunty) was in a very critical stage. I thanked her and disconnected the phone in no time.

I didn't know what I was going to do or say. Whether my presence around her would do any good to her health? We rushed through the reception to the ICUs. Doctors didn't allow us to go any further in the ICU area and when asked how Aunty was, they said very critical. One of her neighbours was also there, his name was Shashank and he worked in a bank. He was in his late 20s.

Shashank interrogated us with questions like who we were, how we were related to Aunty. After a lot of prior thought, I said, 'She's this guy – Aryan's foster Mausi.' My enervated mind came up with something apt. It not only made me free of any blood relation with my to-be-mother-in-law (hopefully) but also made Aryan Tanya's brother, which relieved me like no other thing in this world.

Aryan was stunned but as it was my birthday, he didn't object to it.

After two hours of long wait, doctor came out and informed us that situation was under control. She had got really low BP in the evening and she'd fainted, and faced a heart stroke. It was 1 am, my phone had stopped ringing. Shashank, visibly tired, said to Aryan, 'Now that you, being a relative, are here, I am leaving. My parents would come to see aunty tomorrow morning.'

Hours later, my mother told me that Mrs. Mathur and family were flying down to Delhi.

It took Aunty three hours to gain back the consciousness and doctors asked us – being the only so-called relative around – that we could meet her. I was very nervous about facing her.

I asked Aryan to go inside first and I followed behind him. Aryan greeted Aunty and moved aside, and I came face to face with aunty. Upon seeing her, I experienced an earthquake, my entire body shook in an awkward fear.

The moment she saw me, her pulse rose. I could see her face getting reddish and more until a siren burst and I realized that I was the one responsible for it. She screamed, 'What the hell are you doing here?'

I ran off. Doctors and nurses swarmed in and took control of the situation. I waited outside. Aryan, as though Aunty was not his real Mausi stayed along. Doctors asked Aryan who I was and why did Mrs. Mehra (yes, that's what her surname was) get frenzied on seeing me? We both shrugged as if we didn't know. Doctor advised me not to go inside again.

We both slept on the benches outside, all through the night. Next morning, neighbours flocked in and we left for IIT to freshen up. As soon as I returned to the hospital, this time all alone in the evening, my cellphone buzzed. This time it was an unknown Delhi number. I picked it up expecting a birthday wish, but it was something else.

'Kanav, Mummy got a heart attack Kanav,' Tanya was crying on the other end. She had just arrived in Escorts.

'Turn around,' I said.

She saw me, at first acted as though she was going to hug me, but later realized that Paritosh was standing right next to her. I greeted Mrs. Mathur and asked about Aunty's health.

'She is better, would be discharged the next day,' Mrs. Mathur told me.

'He's Kanav. Mrs. Bajaj's son,' she told Paritosh.

'Do you want to meet Mom? She's been asking me that she had seen you, did I call you and all that. I said that she might have been mistaken. But, you seriously are here,' Tanya said, as we moved to the sides.

'Hmm.'

'Mami later explained to her that she had asked your Mom to help her and that calmed Mom a bit. Mom quizzed her severely about how did Mami know your Mom and you. When satisfied with the answers, she even inquired about how is your Mom – when Mami very eagerly appreciated her. Apparently, her opinion about you has enhanced,' Tanya said.

I went to meet Aunty, along with Tanya. I folded my hand in a *namaste*. She didn't say a word back. She just kept staring at me and after a while she asked, 'You both, stand away from each other.'

I smiled, wished her the best of health and left. Tanya stayed with her Mom for a week and Paritosh took all of them, including her mother, to US for the remaining days of Tanya's education that was slightly more than two months. I didn't disturb Tanya during that time as I realized it was the moment when her mother needed her the most.

Her health got better with time and both of them came back to India finally in late November. Tanya was to begin her job at McKonjee Gurgaon from mid-Dec. My entire attention was to crack McKonjee's interview on day 1, as Tanya had told me that her Mom owing to her failing health wanted to marry her off early and if I didn't make it big – which meant better than Tanya career-wise, my chances would be dim. Tanya and I, concerned about her mother's health, realized that it was not right to go against her in any way because that could have severe impact on her health.

Chapter 23:
DECEMBER 1, 2010

This story is about December 1 - the first day of placements of IIT Delhi.

For the first time in the year 2010, did I wake up before 7 am. For the first time in my four years of engineering, had I taken a bath - so early. Other than occasional shivers, slight panting and feeble 'I-am-so-cool' feeling, I experienced numbness all over.

It was the day of interview. Job interview. My interview with McKonjee and Company was scheduled at 8 o' clock in the morning. In such a cold weather, it sounds pretty insane, isn't it? Well, yes. But you know, good things don't come easy. The company is indeed reputed, with so and so, blah and blah credentials and worldwide standings, by which I was completely wooed, and I still am. So, at 7.00 am sharp, I was completely suited-up, much like Barney once again, except for the awesomeness. I rushed to the interview room, feeling quite tip-top. Other interviewees, some of them my batch-mates, were waiting already. All of them smelled quite good, and some looked as well. Early bath, you see! I was allotted an interviewer, a Sardarji, I don't exactly remember his good name. He was quite scary. No, not by the face or voice, but by his walk. He advanced towards me as if he was gonna give me a head-butt, rather a pugaree-butt. In absolute cold and inviolable lull, I tried to make noise with my newly bought Hush-Puppies, thereby advancing towards him. He anticipated the rhythm and that led to a firm hand-shake. Firmer from my side, just to let him know that I was not scared. Or rather let me know that I wasn't. 'Hello, I'm Kanav,' I said, in a crisp and soft voice.'

'Hi,' he said. Quite frugal. I waited for him to continue, while we advanced towards the slaughter house.

'Your good name please,' I asked. Being curious is considered good, isn't it?

'Hmmm,' he said. That's all he said.

At this point of time, four separate thoughts swayed in my head at the same time.

1. Either he had not heard my question. Quite possible.

2. He could have forgotten his name. He might be trying to recollect.

3. He didn't like me asking his good name. Stern interviewer, you see?

4. His name would not be good at all - something like *Champu* Singh?

Okay, so I was lost in my mind and in his 'hmmm', when he opened the door to the slaughter house. When I saw the room, my mind went completely blank. The four different thoughts merged with each other and made the most amazing potpourri one could ever have. 'Kanav, have a seat,' Hmmm said. Let's call him Hmmm, for ease. I was glad to know that he could actually frame sentences. 'Thanks a lot,' I grabbed the opposite chair, the cold seat for the ready-to-be-slaughtered donkey. My butt froze. Come on, I was wearing cotton trousers for the first time in my college life. I tried to make myself comfortable, but he had some ulterior motives.

'So, you're?' Hmmm shot the trigger straightaway. I was startled.

'I am... I am Kanav Bajaj, student of Engineering Physics, 4th year...'

'No, no, don't go ahead. I just forgot your name. So Kanav, what do you like?' Hmmm asked.

'Definitely not a creepy Sardar in the chilly morning!' I thought.

'Hmmm..,' I said and began thinking in a similar manner to Hmmm. Despite my liking for Hmmm, he didn't seem pleased. I continued, 'I like writing. I like business. And, I like people.'

'What's the order of liking?' He asked.

'The reverse. People, business and writing,' I said. The first big mistake.

'When it's your first choice, then why did it come at last?'

'I saved the best for the last,' I tried to please him with my wit. He didn't know appreciation.

'Hmmm,' he said. I think he liked his name too much. His eyes were deadly.

'Okay, so tell me about this *CrushList.in* that you've mentioned in your resume?' Hmmm asked. No problem, I had plenty.

'So, CrushList.in is my start-up, which I founded around 6 months ago. It caters to people who are shy and can't disclose their crushes that they like them. In this...blah blah blah...blah blah blah.'

'Interesting? You're a writer too...what have you written?' Hmmm developed some interest. His scary eyes turned a bit green.

'I've written a novel, titled "Oops! 'I' fell in love!" which I got published in Aug, 2009. The sequel, 'Ouch! That Hearts..' came out last to last month and has already crossed the 10000 mark.,' I said, quite proudly.

'Are your novels autobiographical?'

'No, they are fictitious. Autobiographies tend to be boring, you know,' I said, casually. My confidence was sky-rocketing.

'Why are you interested in consulting?' Hmmm asked. He was good at changing topics.

The rocket encountered sudden drag. 'Hmmm, consulting is a field which would offer me great insight into the field of business and people, which I'm really passionate about. It would give me a chance to....blah blah blah ... tell me to stop licking your boot, you sucker...blah blah blah.'

He looked convinced. Boot-licking, who doesn't like that - that too at the start of the day?

'You're a writer as well as an entrepreneur. And you're making money too from both the places. If I'd been at your place, I would have pursued the venture full-time. Why don't you go full-time?'

'Is your company all about the money?' I uttered, irritably. 'No, it isn't, at all,' he defended.

'But your idea is good, pursue it.'

'Sir, I'm not making any money from the venture. Yes, I'm earning from my books but that I can earn along with the job, which I desperately want,' I frankly blurted, only to realize later that it would turn costly for me.

'So,' he began with a nefarious smile, 'you are telling me that you want a job only for money, for which as I said, McKonjee doesn't provide.'

I was nonplussed. I didn't know what to do. I didn't know what to say. I cried to Lord Hanuman for help, but it seemed even He got scared of facing the deadly Sardarji. Or maybe, even He was a late riser.

'Thanks for the interview. Great to meet you,' he abruptly said and subtly, respectfully and diplomatically asked me to get lost. 'Hmmm,' I said, in a contemplative tone. I stood up and started walking away. Dejected face of Tanya flashed on my mental canvas and I realized I could not afford to lose the job. I stopped before leaving the slaughter house to beg mercy of the butcher for the one last time.

'Sir, I beg you to select me, otherwise I won't get married, please,' I cried out in agony, 'even my girlfriend is in your company, sir please.' I jumped on his feet and scared the hell out of him. Frightening him turned out to be my only achievement on that day.

He caught hold of my shoulders and said, 'I didn't reject you till now. But you screwed it up Kanav. Our company has this strict policy of not selecting anyone closely related to anyone already recruited in the company. Now we can't select you, Kanav. All the best with your future pursuits.' I left the slaughter house, disappointed, heartbroken and angry at my stupidity. My Mom as well as Tanya couldn't have been more pleased. Both of them did not talk to me till December 7, the lull almost stretched for a week.

The only thing that made me feel good was that Aryan faced the same fate on Day 1 – owing to his lethargy though. He had got shortlisted for the McKonjee interviews and a couple of other companies on the Day 1, but he forgot to get up early in the morning and accidentally skipped his interviews. He was least bothered however, as he chose to play a football match over preparing for interviews in the forthcoming days. He didn't appear in any companies that came later. While, Sameer went to Himalayas for what he said was a spiritual retreat, as he believed that he was much above jobs, though he later got a job with British Gas, which had a good package.

I had no idea about Anuj until a day later, the news that Anuj had cracked a prominent Investment Banking job ran in our hostel corridors. He was so happy that he celebrated with all his past girlfriends at the Hard Rock Cafe – his bill surmounting to 40 thousand rupees – for which he had to resort to Aryan's credit card once again.

Chapter 24:
THE BLOWN JOB

The next 15 days at campus was like walking through fire. What hurt the most was each of my batchmates made it through and got placed in some prominent company. My start-up and novels did no good to my CV and portrayed me as a guy who wouldn't fit in the company's culture. My department Engineering Physics turned out to be the most pathetic branch of IIT, after Textile, as there were no companies willing to take us. They mistook us for MSc Physics and sidelined us saying that we were non-engineers with useless B.Tech degrees.

Adding to all the misery was the fact that Tanya had already started working in McKonjee, New Delhi and she desperately wanted me to get established and meet her mother, owing to her failing health, as she had started searching a groom for her. Though her rancour against me had been dissolved to some extent, but still considering me as a prospective groom for her beautiful and settled daughter was not something that her motherly ego could relent, after she came to know that I was jobless.

21st December
'Hey, come on, why can't you get placed? I understand that you lack face value but at least you are talented.' Tanya said.

'Tell that to the HR department of your company,' I squalled.

'Come on, get a job. Would you like to see me get married to Aryan, who came for interview today at McKonjee through some recommendation?'

She knew how to boil my blood: by mentioning my ace roommate's advances on her.

'Bloody Aryan. They are bound to take him. Didn't he fall asleep in the interview?'

'Don't know. I just met him during lunch, at the cafeteria below our office.'

'What the hell! Help me out. I have been rejected by 23 companies. 23! Some said that they don't find an engineer in me, some say that I'm too creative and emotional, some say that I am the start-up guy and they don't trust me continuing with them for long. I'm planning to go full-time with my venture.'

'Go for it and see me marrying Aryan. You are not making great money with it right now, do it once it becomes bigger,' she advised.

'At least you are making good money. Can't you run my home?' I said.

'But for that, you got to get engaged to me. And for that, you need to ask my mother. And my mother would only agree, if you earn more than me. See yourself, am I not pricey?'

'Damn! Who told you to get into the most elite job on the planet? Could not you take up a job of a stenographer or something?'

'Wow, after graduating from Massachusetts, a job of a typist! That's ambitious thinking, Mr. Penniless Author-turned-Entrepreneur!'

'Damn, at least I could tell her that I'm earning decent royalties from my novel.'

'Don't ever dare. If she gets to read your novels, in which you have made her a villain, she would never agree.'

'She made herself a villain in our lives, not I,' I said, being very particular not to offend her.

'Let me fix something for you. Ruchi had been working in the HR of this company – Devalue Surf, and they might hire you, off-campus.'

'What's the package?'

'Something around 5 lacs,' she said.

'WTF! How would I be competing with you? If I say my novels, I can come equal to you.'

'Don't even dare to speak about that. Instead lie to her that your package is more. She would never get to know. She would cut your head into pieces if she reads that you called her a devil and more in your novels.'

'So ironic. She would become a devil upon reading that she has been compared with a devil,' I said, sarcastically.

'Hey Creep, long time. How are you doing?' Ruchi responded. Tanya had asked me to call her.

'Great! I needed a little help from your end,' I straightaway came to the point. Generally it's mean to call your close friends only about some work, but the good thing with Ruchi was that she would never mind.

'Yes boss! Order please,' she said, in an encouraging tone.

I told her about my deplorable condition and the fact that

Tanya's mother was considering a groom for her. She was stupefied. She couldn't believe my words.

'Come tomorrow, suited, in my Gurgaon office. You have an interview scheduled,' she said, without wasting much time.

She had always been a Messiah. I was speechless, for a while. I thanked her and promised a treat to her at the best bar in Gurgaon, owing to her penchant for vodkas even though I didn't drink.

The next day, I went suited in Devalue Surf Gurgaon Office, and to my surprise, Ruchi wasn't around. She asked her friend, Sunaina to guide me through the interview process.

I was not nervous. After failing in 23 interviews in sequence, one good thing that happens is that you are not afraid to fail again. Sunaina directed me to the interview room, where my HR interview was going to be taken.

I went inside, there was someone sitting in the chair, which was turned to the other side. I couldn't see the face. I coughed and asked, 'May I have a seat?'

'Yes,' a feminine voice answered.

'So, Mr. Kanav, tell me the story of how you got hooked up with your girlfriend Tanya?'

The question blew my mind. I stared blankly. The chair turned around; a lady with big black spectacles greeted me with a mischievous smile. She was strangely familiar. She took off her specs and I gaped in bewilderment.

'Ruchi? Oh my God!' The incredibility of the moment left me totally stunned.

It was the most amazing interview of my life. We chatted about everything that had passed in the last two years; it was an interview with coffee table gossips littered all over. I was meeting Ruchi after two years, though she had constantly been in touch with Tanya in the last few days ever since she joined the Gurgaon Office. Ruchi had lost her weight and looked like a corporate woman – intellectual, elegant and dignified. My interview went for over an hour, until our stories lasted.

'Don't you have to go back to work?' I asked.

'This is work. I'm interviewing you,' she winked at me.

Another quick interview, with the Partner of the firm followed, where my confidence peaked thanks to the lovely environment that Ruchi had created earlier and I easily glided through it. Two hours later, when I was sipping coffee with Tanya at her cafeteria during her lunch time, my cell-phone rang.

I was hired. No more interviews. No more disappointment. I got so excited that I kissed Tanya on her cheeks and made a spectacle of us in front of all her co-workers, a faux pas she had never forgiven – not even till now. She slapped me back for it, in front of everyone. But later she said sorry as well. She apparently liked the surprise. I am going to do it once again, very soon. *Yes, I'm wicked.*

I was in another world. I felt so relieved as though the burden of Mt.Everest had been removed from my shoulders. I immediately asked Tanya if she could fix up my meeting with her Mom. She relented and asked me to meet her the next day.

Chapter 25:
THE INTERVIEW WITH THE VILLAIN

Two hours before going to meet the lady of my nightmares along with the lady of my dreams, I was tad nervous. I was wrong about no more interviews. This was going to be the major one. I couldn't even imagine failing in it.

I dressed myself as well as I could, didn't use musk to prevent the streak of sneezes from my beloved, shaved my cheek of every strand of hair to look elegant and suited myself to look settled. I was going to talk about my marriage, without the knowledge of my parents.

Aryan had brought a Skoda from his rich Dad especially to drop me to my in-laws' place, a gesture that required appreciation, but I was trapped in another fear.

'First promise me that you are not going to come out and talk to her mother,' I pleaded to Aryan. I feared if she met Aryan, she would get completely awed by his pleasing personality and would choose him as a groom for Tanya, and with the intensity that Tanya used to poke me about Aryan, I didn't even trust Tanya fully(she would kill me for writing that bit about trust).

When I was ready to leave my hostel on Aryan's car, I called Tanya. I was given four very direct advices, failing which

I could have landed myself in trouble.

1. Don't talk about your novels.

2. Don't disclose your real salary.

3. Don't crack jokes. You suck at it.

4. When in house, don't try to take my help. Being independent all her life, she likes men who are independent and brave, unlike you.

I was hopeful to easily follow the first two guidelines, but I'd never had the practice of the third one and considering the quality of my jokes, I feared that I would be mercilessly butchered, if not by the irate mother, then her daughter. And about the fourth one, I replied to Tanya, 'When I chose to be brave, she sent you to the other side of globe.'

I reached their place, checked out the garage where the very same old fiat was parked whose headlights had once darkened my life. The circular headlights were haughtily staring at me as though asking me to salute them. I spat on them and moved ahead with a victorious smile.

I pressed the call bell. Aunty (from now on, I'll refer to her as Aunty, as now it's become a homely matter for me) opened the door with her typical cold face staring hard at mine. At first, I got so frightened, that I mumbled an indistinct sorry for pressing the call bell. She replied, 'what?' Thereafter, I gathered control over myself and said *namaste* with folded hands. It was only after I said that *namaste* that I was asked to come inside. Just saying.

I got seated on the sofa and began staring around. Aunty came with a lot of snacks.

'I made *gulab jamuns* for you. Tanu told me that you like it,' she said, very calmly. Her cold face exhibited some warmth.

I gladly took a couple of them when she asked me to take more. I felt like a *bali-ka-bakra* once again, this time being fed till neck before getting cut. There were marvelous impressionistic paintings on the wall, where I noticed the signature which said: *P. Mehra*, aunty's name. I exclaimed, 'wow' on seeing the painting of a rickshaw puller in the rain. It was part genuine appreciation and part flattery. She said thanks and told that Tanya also painted, as she showed me a portrait of an old woman that was made by her.

I was awed. Tanya had never talked about her art to me. I hadn't talked about my sister's art to her, either. Perhaps, each one of us had thought that the other person would be disinterested in art and that's why there was no mention. Moreover, she wasn't a self-obsessed jerk like me to boast of her talent. The memory of Sakshi Singh, the artist I'd once dated came back and I was proud to realize that Tanya could give her a tough competition.

Just then, Tanya arrived from her room. Her wet hair and freshness told me that she had just come from her bath.

'So Mr. Bajaj, what brings you here?' Aunty shot her first arrow.

Mr. Bajaj! Was it a compliment for my sleek attire or was it subtle mockery?

'Aunty...' I fumbled with words. It was as though my tongue was walking on a steep road of a Mario-like video game with a lot of words in the air that it had to jump and acquire, but instead it toppled and rolled across the slope, without encountering any words.

'Aunty...ahem ahem,' I coughed, looking at Tanya, who hinted me to go ahead and break the awkward pause.

'Aunty,' it was the third time I was saying that word and I

felt like pulling my tongue out and hanging myself with it tied to the ceiling fan. Aunty was now irritated, her head clearly showed wrinkles and she was about to speak something, when I nervously sped through my monologue:

'I want to marry your daughter. I mean not now, but in a while, but I want you to stop searching a daughter for her, umm.. I mean, a groom for her. I'm perfect for her. She also likes me. You also know that, don't you?'

She didn't reciprocate and with her sharp look, I could understand that I'd erred of woofing like a dog in a lion's den. I was waiting for the lion to roar.

'What's your age?' She asked sternly.

'21. Would be turning 22 in two months,' I said, by now becoming very comfortable.

'Are you older than her?' She asked. I was euphoric; it felt as though she was matchmaking with our *janam-patri* in her head.

'Yes,' I replied excitedly, '2 months'.

'Then you should be earning more than her.'

'Umm, yes,' I lied, in synergy with the advice that Tanya gave me before arriving there. Nervously, I picked up one more *gulab jamun*.

'Keep that *gulab-jamun* down,' she hollered, 'I am talking to you, isn't it? Should you be eating while having a conversation?'

I kept the plate down, with my trembling hands. *One shouldn't have a conversation while eating.* I kept thinking how she had turned the statement that was in my favour, against me. Unable to trace anything, I stammered a mild sorry.

'Say sorry to yourself. You would have coughed otherwise,' her motherly side was back.

'So where was I?' she asked.

I had no idea. I had forgotten during her intense reprimand. Thankfully, Tanya was around.

'Then you should be earning more than her,' Tanya said.

'Yes. So my next question is: tell me what Tanya's salary is?'

'12 lacs p.a,' I said. This was by far the worst interview I'd ever been into. I didn't have any idea why I so desperately wanted to be crushed like a mosquito under that interviewer for life, by marrying her daughter. No wonder love is blind.

'So yours should be over 12 p.a. Is it?' She said. No wonder she was the mother of an Economics graduate.

'Yes,' I lied.

'Where do you work?' She asked.

'Devalue Surf. Though I'm going to begin it after six months' I said.

'What vague name is that for a company? Does it sell detergents?'

'It's a knowledge processing outsourcing company,' I said.

'Okay okay,' she said, impressed with my corporate vocabulary.

'What's your career's plan? Where do you see yourself in a few years?' She asked me.

'I see myself as a celebrated writer,' I said naturally, without thinking twice. Tanya turned back her face; aunty suddenly lost all the aunty-like charisma from her persona and looked like she was going to kick me out of their place.

'Sorry, that was just out of the blue,' I tried to rectify myself, but aunty sensed something that was being concealed from her, for a long time.

'Do you write?' She asked.

'Yes,' I said.

'What have you written so far?' She asked, this time visibly interested.

'Blogs. Articles for newspapers,' I lied about the latter part.

'Which newspaper? What kind of articles?'

'College Newspaper: Campus Rumpus. I wrote about hostel politics.'

'That must be online. Let me search. I have always been interested in reading. Reading tells you a lot about the author. What's your entire name?'

'Kanav Bajaj,' I said. For the first time, someone googling my name didn't give me pride, but instead made me full of fear and shame. She took her iPAD residing next to her and googled my name.

The first link that came when she typed my name was Flipkart's book link: 'Oops! I fell in love!' by Kanav Bajaj. She was shocked. She showed it to me and asked, 'Wait a minute, what's this?' My interview turned out to be a stress interview for me.

'That must be some other Kanav Bajaj,' I retorted. I was so tied up in the shackles of lies that I'd created that I had no options other than tricking her into the same.

'The introduction says: Kanav Bajaj is a student of IIT Delhi. What's going on?' She oppugned. I had no answer.

'I'm sorry for lying,' I said; my eyes filled with tears.

'What's there to feel bad about? You are a novelist. That's something you should be proud of.'

She said and ordered my book, cash on delivery. It was the first book order that I was going to repent.

'Mom, so would you stop searching for a groom for me.

You do find Kanav good enough for me, don't you?' Tanya said.

'No. Not too soon. Let me first read his books and assess. As I said, what you write gives a very clear idea about what you think.'

Tanya didn't expect that. She was baffled. I was on the verge of a nervous breakdown.

'Aunty, that book isn't meant for people your age.'

'What do you mean? Do I look old to you?' She asked, with a haughty smirk.

'No, I didn't mean that. I was just telling you that this book is for youngsters, especially college students. It's not literature.'

'Who reads literature nowadays? Everybody reads Chetan Bhagat now, and hopefully, after I recommend your books to my kitty friends, they would start reading you. Wow, I'll feel great to boast!' She said childishly. It was the first time she had wished something good for me and ironically, even that made me feel suicidal.

'Tch tch,' I tussled with mortification, and said, 'Aunty, I think I would be leaving now. *Namaste.*'

'*Beta*, at least have dinner,' she said. She had referred to me as *Beta* for the first time and it made me more susceptible to feel like a *bali-ka-bakra*.

'Next time Aunty. I have some work.'

'Yes, the next time. I'll give you a critique of your book.'

I had performed miserably in my interview, though my image in Aunty's mind had been uplifted but I could feel that it's delusional and the moment she reads all the stuff written about her in my book, I was going to be strangled with the barbed wires circumscribing her house.

I moved out, Aunty sent Tanya to escort me till the gate.

'Jerk! Why did you talk about your book?' Tanya screamed, as soon as she came outside.

'Stop shouting at me! I love writing. I'm not going to keep lying about something that I love,' I yelled. I was vexed with the experience.

'Stop being such a girl! Leave that to me. I know you love writing and I'm not asking you to lie. I just wanted you to not tell her that. Now she'll find out who the villain of your first book is and God only knows what will happen thereafter!' She said maturely.

'Oh God, why did I fall in love with this jerk? He can't even be diplomatic for me,' she cried, looking up at the skies. A swarm of pigeons which was returning home at dusk in the sky answered her query by pooping on her head. I jested with uncontrollable laughter, shouting, 'God answered! God answered,' gratefully looking up at the pigeons.

A minute later, the last few pigeons of the lot, threw their answer even at me, this time sadly on my face. It was now her turn to keep laughing.

'Devil answered. Devil answered,' she squeaked.

'I was better off inside the den with Aunty rather than in between wild animals like Tanya outside.'

'Come on in,' she said.

'Now, I'll enter only as your groom. Hope Aunty doesn't get the chance to read my book,' I said before I boarded an auto-rickshaw for IIT, from just outside Tanya's home.

'Sir, are you not the same person who sold me perfumes long ago?' The *autowala* chirped.

I carefully checked his face. Even he was looking at me.

Yes, he was the same guy. The same person I hired years ago, for my first date, and traded my perfumes with him, when I realized that I'd lost my wallet.

'No, which person?' I lied, hesitantly.

'Even your voice has not changed, sir. You hired this auto from IIT itself,' he said, speeding his auto across the same bus stand where I'd once spent a lonely night.

'Did you get to meet your girl?' He went on, ignoring me.

'What bullshit are you talking about?' I said, and before undergoing any further interrogation,

'Stop the auto. I said stop the auto,' I shouted him to stop his vehicle, but he kept ignoring me.

'This is not an auto sir, this is *ramdulari*, my girlfriend,' he winked at me from the rear view mirror. I felt so angry that I grabbed his neck from behind and shouted, 'Asshole, I said stop the bloody auto.'

'Call it Ramdulari sir, I'll stop it,' he reverted. He increased his speed. I left his neck.

'Stop this – *ramdulari* or whatever her name is!' I pleaded. The vehicle halted after making shrill noise. I gave him a 500 rupees note and asked him to change it for me.

'I know you are the same guy sir. Aren't you?'

'Yes, I'm the same guy. Does it make you happy? Now give me back the change,' I cried.

'See, I told you *Ramdulari*, that he's the same guy. Sorry sir, I don't have change, but I do have something else.'

He stood up, turned around and opened his seat cushion. I was frightened, thinking him to take out some revolver and I started running away.

'Sir, wait. Here is the change,' he shouted. I turned around. I was confused by what I saw. He had bottles: two distinct perfume bottles in his hand.

'Sir, these are your bottles. You traded them with me for 200 rupees, remember? I didn't use it since my Ramdulari doesn't like its smell. Please take it and keeping in mind the inflation, I keep the change. *Ab hisaab clear,*' he said happily. He handed them to me and I stood there, holding those two bottles, perplexed and dumbstruck.

He restarted the auto and started going away. Seeing no auto around, I yelled once again, '*Ramdulari!*' and he halted.

'Now that you have got your *hisaab* clear, drop me to IIT,' I said and got seated. Reminiscence of my first date came running by and I related the story of my first novel to him, which he heartily enjoyed and dropped me back to the lap of my alma mater, without any further assault of my wallet.

Chapter 26:
THE DEADLY WAIT

The last semester at IIT Delhi is very different from the previous semesters. The number of bottles of booze exceeds the number of hours in a day. Classes are replaced by research projects, where soon to be engineers exercise their lethargy, fraudulence and googling ability in the name of original research.

I had just one lecture course which was on literature, as I hoped that it would help me improve my writing. Unknowingly, my professor had got to know that I'd written a novel and don't know why, that made her despise me quite evidently. Whenever I used to go to her class, she used to very subtly insult me by taunting, 'sir would you like to take a class on literature? A 100 rupee literature?' making the entire class scoff at me.

I used to feel so humiliated that I stopped attending her class. I really feared that she would fail me intentionally in my exam and extend my degree.

One day, after I missed more than 12 classes in a row owing to my second book launch and its repercussion in the campus, my professor called for me in her cabin, through one of my regular friends. I thought that now that I was not attending her classes, she wanted to insult me privately.

'May I come in Ma'am?' I asked her. I was standing at the door.

After inspecting me from top to bottom, she asked me to come in and get seated.

'Ma'am you had called me,' I reminded her.

'Yes, I'd something important to tell you.'

'Yes, Ma'am.'

'If you miss one more class, you will be declared failed in the course.'

'I would come from the next class, Ma'am.'

'I didn't intend that. I want you to miss the next class,' she said.

I was puzzled. She was asking me to fail. After being meek and submissive for so long, I could not take more.

'What do you want from me? When I come to your class, you mock me. When I don't, you ask my friends to call me. When I'm promising that I would be coming to your class, you say that you want me to miss the next class.'

'Well, this is what I'd wanted from you. To see that the confident and angry side of you exists. You kept assimilating my sarcasm all along, without ever responding, getting angry from within. I wanted you to retort, to respond to my sarcasm in real – because as a writer, you'd been too introverted, never exercising your freedom of speech.'

'That's because I'd been taught by my parents to respect my elders.'

'Your parents or your girlfriend?' She took my 2nd book *Ouch! That 'hearts'..* out from her drawer and placed that on the table.

'Now, once again you are trying to embarrass me. Go on,' I asked irritably.

'No, not this time. Congratulations. I liked your book,' she said, and continued, 'I want you to represent IIT Delhi Literature Department in the Jaipur Literature Festival next week.'

'What about the attendance?'

'It's already cent percent,' she handed over the attendance sheet. I was baffled after seeing all present. Grateful tears filled my eyes and I smiled.

'All the best,' she said and handed over the business class flight tickets from Delhi to Jaipur. I was overwhelmed, in courtesy, I touched her feet, when she said, 'come on, I'm not as old as you think.'

A week later, I was at Jaipur. It was the most enriching part of my college life as I got to meet my favorite writers like Gulzar sahib, Girish Karnad and Vikram Seth. Two months later, I secured the highest grade in the literature class and Madam has become my lifelong mentor.

Apparently, as I'd hoped, Tanya's mother, though she got my book, didn't get an opportunity to read it. Her relatives – Paritosh and family – had come to their place on a vacation and all day, she would be busy in daily chores.

However, that didn't stop her from searching grooms for Tanya, since she was paranoid that she wasn't going to be there for long. She even got Paritosh and Mami involved in the groom-search. Every Sunday Tanya used to be given numerous photos to select one she would like to meet. Though aunty knew about Tanya having an inclination for me but she still hoped that Tanya would find a better groom than me. Tanya, owing to aunty's bad health, didn't debate much and just kept reminding that she had to read my novels and get back to me. In the meantime, she used to doodle on all the photos and made them look cartoonish.

One Saturday, she came to meet me and showed me all the pictures of her prospective bridegrooms.

'Some of them are even uglier than you,' she taunted me.

'How many are better than me?' I asked.

'Around 99%.'

'Why don't you choose them over me then?'

'I would. I'm just waiting for my Mom to finish your novel and rip you off my fate.'

'Great thoughts. If every girlfriend in this world thought like you then there would have been only girls left on this planet.'

'All men would have gone to hell,' she grinned.

'Hell would be on earth,' I sharply replied. She had no answer. I had won.

Sameer came into my room after a long time, to catch up with what was going on in regard to my engagement.

'Do you need any help?' He asked, in a hermit like tone.

'Yes. Get me married, fatty *baba*,' I folded my hands and mock-prayed to him.

'*Avashya*,' he replied.

'Is the villain still your Sasu ma?' He asked.

'Yup.'

'I quit. Don't ask me for any help, *vats*, because your Sasu-ma had taken all my divine powers.'

'It's okay, fatty *baba*. Just grab a seat and tell me what is going on with you? Any chance encounters with the fairer sex, now that you are the Brand Ambassador of British Gas (BG).'

'What? I had broken up long ago and had decided that I would not be dating any other girl, when I decided to become a hermit. I'm even leaving BG for the same.'

'What? When did you decide to become a hermit? Are you out of your mind? You got a wonderful job offer from British Gas, the latter part of the name suits your personality even and you are eager to quit it?' I cried.

'Dude, you know me. I want to be a motivational guru and in India, until and unless one gets some religious stamp on one's identity, people don't take that seriously.'

'That's not true. There are management gurus even, who are treated equally well as spiritual hermits. They haven't been hermits.'

'You won't understand. Leave it. I have recently got associated with this wonderful society called as the Art of Life, and I see that as the best career option. It attracts so many upper class people in it that I will have a huge network of big people all across India who would help set me up as a motivational speaker in their corporate houses.'

'Wow, that's actually strategic. Your society is indeed quite popular. I heard that they have nice girls as well.'

'Yes. That's the flipside of the coin. You are a hermit, with a female fan following.'

'Just get rid of your paunch and you would be the new Swami Sexanand.'

He grinned. I didn't take his words seriously. Most of the time, he kept planning random stuff. Considering his modest family background, I predicted he would go for the British

Gas job offer which had a terrific package and he would make himself comfortable.

Meanwhile, finding my hostel door open, Anuj joined us as well.

'So fuckers, what's up? How's your CrushList going on, Kanav?'

'Nothing great man. It's traffic has stagnated. I realized a serious problem in it: people use it only twice – once while they are listing their crushes and second time, when they get a crush notification. People don't visit it often.'

'That's a serious problem. Did you think of any solution?'

'All the solutions that keep coming to my mind are networking based solutions and with facebook being the big fish, there is not much left to do networking with.'

'What are you up to?' I asked.

'I'm going to Mumbai. Deutsche Bank has called me, with business class flight tickets.'

'Wow. Amazing. Now that you are going into a bank, you have to keep financing us,' Sameer said.

'Why not Fatty, anything for you, except food and drinks,' Anuj retaliated.

'Kanav, Aryan told me that you are getting married. Are you fucking out of your minds?'

'Not married, but engaged, that too with a very rare chance.'

'Who marries so early? Haven't you and Tanu got bored of each other.'

Ever since Anuj got to know that Tanu was none other than my Tanya, he started calling her by her pet-name Tanu. He still carries the ambigram that I made for him and Tanu in his pocket, in hope that someday somebody named Tanu might come across him. However, he still was having an on and off relationship with his latest girlfriend – I forgot what her name was.

'Aunty is not keeping well. She wants to finalize her groom before…' I paused, in search for euphemistic words.

'…she gets finalized. By the way, aunty! Wow, you have become courteous,' Anuj completed my sentence.

'Yes, I have. After all I'm in the company of a saint,' I said and pointed towards Sameer. He winced at me, cursing me for telling his plan to mockery master Anuj.

'Have you become a saint, fatso? Or a thug?' Anuj began his taunts.

'Chuck it,' Sameer said and rushed out of the room.

Anuj with nothing left to do, began philosophizing.

'What will I do with so much money – 14 lacs per annum?'

'Make poor friends like me jealous?' I said, and flashed an irritated look.

'Come on. You'd been making us jealous for over three years now. First by writing a bestseller and getting so much female following, and then, hooking up with the prettiest girl I'd ever seen. And now, you are making us more jealous, by getting engaged to her – crushing every hope in our eyes for a future break-up.'

'Ha-ha. Really? You wished for a break-up?' I asked.

'As if you didn't know. Every guy who has met Tanu wished she could be his. You are a lucky dog, bitch!' He complimented me in his unique style.

'Thank God, I saved her from wolves.'

Chapter 27:
THE JUDGMENT DAY

By now, my patience had given up. I'd started asking Tanya to ask Aunty to come to a conclusion about me, but she would not relent, saying that she did not want to give any kind of pressure on her mother, otherwise her health might degrade. That was the reason she never proclaimed that she was very eager to be with me and just kept rejecting every marriage proposal that came to her, finding one flaw after other.

I thought maybe it was time to get my strongest weapon out. I called my mother and explained the situation to her. I told her about Tanya and she immediately recalled her New York experience.

'Mom, you remember Tanu, don't you?'

'Yes, I liked her, rather loved her. And I also know about you two.'

'What? How come?' I was stunned. Rather than I playing the role of a bashful young man disclosing about his girlfriend to his mother, my mother gave me a stunner with the coolness she admitted that she already knew about Tanya and me.

'What do you think – why did I schedule the lunch at Mrs. Mathur place the next day to Niagara?'

'I don't know. You were friends to her, that's why.'

'No, that was not the reason. She mentioned about her niece Tanya Mehra staying with them, who came from LSR, last year. I immediately realized that she was your Tanya – our Tanya. And when I saw her, my doubt became surety as I could just figure out that the beauty that you described in your novel couldn't have been any different.'

'What? Don't tell me that Ma!' I shouted. I couldn't believe what she said.

'Son, I'm your mother. When you were busy with *oops* in your life, I was already at *ouch*.'

'What about Dad, Mom?'

'Your Dad likes her too; I showed him her photo, from that day. We call her *bahu* already.'

'What? Are you out of your minds?' I was dumbfounded.

'We were just waiting for you to admit the same,' she said. I realized that God had been too kind on me to give me such cool parents.

'Now you people are already eager to set me off into marriage, I have a request for you.'

'Sure, go on.'

'Call Mrs. Mathur now on her India's no. 9974xxxxxx and ask for my *rishta*. Tanya's mother has been searching for a groom all the while and if delayed, I would be history in their lives.'

I sincerely doubted what effect would the presence of Paritosh had on their decisions. My mother was quick at the task. She immediately called at their number and asked for Mrs. Mathur. After inquiring the general whereabouts and well-being, she immediately nudged the bull's eye.

She explained that I am settled and I liked Tanya, and even

Tanya liked me. She asked her to please butter her sister in-law a little, endorsing me. I was so grateful to my mother that I promised her that I would eat *Chyawanprash* daily, an advice that I still follow.

Around ten minutes later, Tanya called me. I picked up the phone and excitedly shouted, 'My Mom did it. Now it's your Mom's turn.'

'It's all screwed up,' her voice was broken, as though she was crying. I became really tense.

'Mama has this friend in London and he has recommended his son for me.'

'Then reject him. It's simple.'

'I can't reject him.'

'Why?' My pillars of hope had been shaken from their foundation.

'Because he is really handsome,' she said and burst out laughing.

'You almost killed me…' I said.

'Aww, poor baby.'

'I didn't complete my sentence. I was saying: You almost killed me… with joy,' I retorted.

'Jerk!'

'Did your Mami speak to your Mom?'

'Not yet, but she asked me whether I liked you.'

'What did you say?'

'Obviously…no,' she said and started laughing once again.

'I said yes and she smiled and said, "Even I found him good last time" and went away,' Tanya said.

'Wow, your relatives are so good.'

'Don't say that too soon. Mom has given your book to Paritosh and he might be calling you for an interview very soon. You are going to get raped, in front of me. Devil laughter. Muahaha.'

'Are you serious?' I asked, shivering.

'Yes. Sorry. You should have thought before writing all those metaphors about my family.'

'It's okay. But let me remind you my dear lady that it has instances where you were hurling abuses at Paritosh.'

'Damn! Wait, I'll say that it's all fictitious.'

A day later, the much awaited call came. Tanya told me that everybody – right from Paritosh, Aunty to Mami had gone through my books. They didn't opinionate till now in front of Tanya and were seriously waiting to meet me.

'All of them get pretty fierce opinions about every small thing in the world. So don't mind if you are ragged too harshly.'

'Won't you help me in anyway?'

'Remember the last time I tried to help you in the garage, I was grounded for the next three years. Though now she appreciates my independence, but still I don't want to shoot up her blood pressure especially when she is not keeping well. Nothing precedes her health, for me,' she said in an apologetic tone.

'I appreciate.'

Three hours later

The entire ambiance was unwelcoming for me. Surprisingly, I wasn't feeling nervous. It was the Judgment Day for me. I'd to come out victorious and hence, there was no way to get daunted by their serious looks.

Paritosh was sitting in front of me, his black-rimmed spectacle sitting on his little nose. Mrs. Mathur was standing behind him, with a trifle hint of a smile on her face. But that didn't make me happy, since the anecdote about her rubbing red chillies on little Divya's teeth when she asked the meaning of word sex kept whirling in my mind. Aunty was sitting next to me, with her chin resting on her folded hands.

Tanya was peering from inside her room, hiding behind the curtains. Her eyes crossed mine twice and tried to scare me away. The pin-drop silence that prevailed for over a minute was suddenly broken by Divya(Lulu) running towards me, 'Hello bhaiya, you visited us at our place in US isn't it? I didn't tell anyone about....'

If there was one moment when I ever felt the need of having a suicide button on my mobile phone, it was that. My tongue was out and head swung to and fro to stop Lulu from saying the next word. All the remaining eyes in the room were expectantly looking at her to come to know another dirty secret of mine. I was sweating profusely. I just prayed to my eternal enemy – God – to save me, by either stopping her or by either stopping my heartbeats. Neither of that happened. Lulu continued.

'I didn't tell anyone about the curtain that you were fixing,' she said in an adorable American accent and sat next to me.

I exhaled deeply. A loud sigh was heard from near the door, where Tanya was standing, but she immediately went inside and started coughing, desperately trying to sound real. I wished she managed to. I grabbed Lulu with my arms, and after catching my breath and reclaiming my lost confidence, I mumbled, 'how are you Lulu? I remember the curtain that I had accidentally broken. Thank you for not telling it to anyone.'

The eyes that looked eager to see me naked had been left to stare aimlessly, after things didn't go as they'd hoped. I was once again attacked by their powerful stares and the awkward lull.

'So Aunty, how are you?'

'I was fine.'

'Was? What does that mean?'

'That means that I was fine but I'm not, after reading your book.' Her face had become red with anger. 'What piece of filth did you write about me?'

'Aunty, please calm down, it's not good for your health,' I said. Mr. and Mrs. Mathur also assisted in calming her down.

'Aunty, I asked you not to read. It was not for you,' I calmly said.

'You know what Paritosh, this kid who has no manners and respect for elders, who is sitting right across me, wants to marry my daughter. How dare he? Your book was not for me. Similarly, Tanya is not for you. Get out of my house,' she thundered, pointing at me. Tanya came out running seeing her mother in an unmanageable condition and held her tightly.

I was awestruck, having no idea what to do or say next.

'Kanav, get out,' Tanya screamed at me. My presence was shooting her blood pressure up. 'Move out Kanav, get out of her sight.'

'That guy who calls me demon and so many other vile things wants to marry my daughter. Damn him!' She kept assaulting my self-respect as she was taken inside and I couldn't help notice. I started moving out. Tanya and Mrs. Mathur took her in the adjacent room.

Paritosh followed up with me. This was the first time I would be hearing him speak. He had a slightly feminine voice – shrill like a cuckoo and the bass was like a cacophonous frog.

'Hey, sorry for what happened. I thought that *Didi* would be having a serious conversation but she lost her temper. We all read your novels and though, personally, I would say that you are a good writer, but you should not have written offensive things about her – a character that exists in the real world. And, just by reading your exact description of her, we were shocked to conclude that whatever has been written in your books about you and Tanya is real, is it?'

'Not at all. It's a parody on my love story. Only the climax of the first novel is inspired from the real life event. Everything else was fictitious,' I lied.

'How sure are you?'

'100%. You can ask Tanya about it even.'

'We don't want to involve the daughter of our house in such petty things,' he said exasperatedly. In that one sentence, I could sense that he had the similar short-temper as his sister. I observed his face carefully; it was very similar to aunty. Demonish. I decided that I won't look at him again.

'Kanav, my mother wants to talk to you,' Tanya rushed to me.

'Yes,' I went inside. I just wished to God: if I were to be electrocuted inside, then please make it fast. I didn't want to have a painfully slow death.

'So you called me a lunatic, buffoon, angry old woman, jerk and even hurled cusses at me in your second book,' she was going through the pages of my novel. She had highlighted the places where she had been verbally attacked.

'You didn't even bother to change the names. See, Paritosh he's written your name as well and called you mean ass. Thank God that you didn't know my name else you would have made shameless puns on that,' she said.

I asked Tanya later about her mother's name, when she told: *Padma*. Though I would have loved to make puns on that particular word since it had too much scope of punning, but since she was elder to me, I probably wouldn't have. Or might have, depending on the level of the angst that I carried for the torture that I faced in the past.

Suddenly, the words of my Professor of Literature at IIT came crawling to me. 'I wanted to see the real writer in you, the expressive rather than introverted Kanav.'

'You know what Aunty? By making a fuss out of all that, you are just confirming the use of all the words had been apt. Had I not taken a personal story as an inspiration, and if you had read my novel, you would have just enjoyed it thoroughly. Ask anyone, let Mrs. Mathur answer. Knowing that there were no major characters based on you, did you not enjoy my novel?'

She nodded. Aunty got enraged. 'Nita, you too?' For the first time I came to know that Mrs. Mathur even had a first name. She nodded once again. It was my first taste of triumph at her den.

'What should I say now?' Her rage climbed up the charts and she completely blew it a moment later, when she uttered with rancour, 'When my own family is going against me, who should I trust? First my daughter fell for this insolent bastard and now my relatives.'

'Mom, mind your words.' It was the first time I heard Tanya speaking loudly against her mother. And it was that time, when if she hadn't spoken, I would have never come to her house again. She only had taught me that respect precedes love, and this time, her mother had crossed her limits.

'Just because I have been very obedient, nice and caring for the last two years doesn't mean that you can go on and on about anything, Kanav had just called you a lunatic or a demon but you crossed your limits today by using that filthy word at him. Do you even realize that you are alive today because of him? If he really carried hatred against you during your last heart-stroke, he would have never come to help you at the hospital. You hate him just because you can't accept the fact that this guy cares for your daughter much more than all those losers who you have found out. And if you really read his novel, didn't you realize how much do we both value respect. You know what, Kanav and I had been in a relationship for over 4 years and we could have done so many filthy things that other immature kids do, but we were always in control and our intention was always very pure of never hurting you. Maybe you couldn't appreciate his care or respect or love, but at least you can appreciate my happiness. He never wanted to go against my family, but rather wanted to win your heart,' Tanya's voice choked as she reached the end of her monologue.

Aunty broke into tears. It would have been the first time she had heard somebody louder than her in her entire life. She sat on the ground and started wailing like a baby, we all sat around her. Even Tanya was sobbing.

'Aunty, I'm sorry. I love your daughter and believe me when I say that I have immense respect for you. I just want you to treat me as you'd have treated another prospective groom who would have come for your daughter, instead of judging me over my past actions. I'd been very dumb aunty.'

'Not dumb. Jerk!' Aunty said, pointing at the highlighted word *jerk* of my novel that set out a riotous laughter in the room that scared Lulu so much that now she started crying.

'I am so happy to see that my daughter has become so mature. I am sorry for whatever I said, Kanav,' Tanya would later tell me that it was the only time she'd ever said sorry to anyone.

'I'd been a jerk!' Aunty said with a mischievous smile on her face. She had found the word funny. No wonder it was given to me by her daughter.

It was Mrs. Nita Mathur turn to speak up. She had been holding a secret in her mind all the while. '*Didi*, I have met her mother in the US. She is such a lively lady and she even called me today, she wanted to talk to you, but I didn't give you as I sensed that you were not in your perfect mood.'

'Call your mother, Kanav,' Aunty ordered me. I looked at Tanya for an answer, since I was confused. She hinted me to follow Aunty's command – an act that I feared because it could turn disastrous. Two electrodes talking to each other.

'*Namaste*, Mrs. Bajaj. This is Mrs. Mehra this side. Tanu's mother,' she spoke and switched on the speaker for us to listen. I felt a little bit hopeful.

'*Namaste*. How is your health now? I heard about your heart-stroke, I got really worried about it. Hope my useless son had been of some help. Please eat healthy. I will tell you some important vegetarian soups which are good for heart.' My mother began her unidirectional *Chyawanprash* talk.

'Thank you so much. I am calling you to make a little complain to you,' she said.

I was nervous. So was my mother. So were Tanya and everyone else in the room, except Lulu who was busy playing with her taller bicycle, this time.

'Your son, who I testify is a very talented writer, is not a fair person. He is very biased,' Aunty said.

'Biased? What wrong has he done now?' My Mom asked, concerned. The 'now' in her question confirmed that I was the king of wrong doings.

'He's very biased towards you, Mrs. Bajaj. All throughout his novels, he has appreciated and admired you but failed to do so for his to-be mother-in-law.'

I could not believe what I'd heard. I looked at Tanya; even she was baffled, together with the other two people in the room. Tears of joy welled up in my eyes and I unconsciously inched my hands towards Tanya's when Aunty slapped me hard on my hand, and shrieked, 'Move away.'

'Yes, Mrs. Bajaj. To-be-mother-in-law. As my health is not being up to the mark, I wanted to get Tanya engaged before any mishap happens.'

'*Shubh shubh boliye* Mrs. Mehra, *mare apke dushman*,' my mother said.

For a while I looked around, praying for the archaic ceiling fan to not fall on my head to fulfill my mother's last wish. Nothing happened. I got relaxed realizing that I was no more her *dushman*.

'But I have a condition. A very serious condition,' Aunty said dramatically. She added so many layers of suspense that only a murder seemed to be left in the end.

'What?' My mother questioned, puzzled. She was not the kind of a person who could appreciate suspense. She wanted to get to the core of the issue immediately, that's why she gave birth to an engineer.

'That he has to write the third part of the trilogy and transform my image from a villain to a savior in it before marrying my daughter. How else would I be able to boast his authorship in my kitty-circles, tell me?'

'Ha-ha. Absolutely,' my mother chuckled. Tanya and I sighed in relief.

'You know what the best thing about his novel is?'

'Your daughter?' My mother replied. She was smart; no wonder where my smartness comes from.

'Aha! Not exactly where I was heading. The best thing was he didn't change characters' real life names, now if he writes good things about my character, I can make claims that he means those for me,' she said. I had never seen her as happy before. Tanya later echoed my opinion which surprised me, for she related that she had never seen her so happy in the last 14 years that she could remember.

She disconnected the call after scheduling a common get together for both families the next month, during my convocation.

'Thank you Aunty,' I said, touching her feet for blessings, and inched closer to Tanya.

'It's not over yet.'

'I have one more condition.'

'Oh God, Momma!' Tanya cried.

'No kissing, No hugging. No touching. Until you guys are…'

'Engaged,' I shouted delightedly.

'Married,' she retorted, with a haughty smile and continued: 'now you can go.'

It was abrupt. But abruptness was a tradition in their family.

Before leaving, I turned to Tanya, and said, 'want to become a runaway bride?' and before Aunty could change her decision about me, I dashed out of her home, stopping for a moment to kiss her Fiat's headlight, and made the swiftest possible exit.

EPILOGUE

Two years later.

Yes, we couldn't kiss for two years. I am just kidding, trying to please my Sasu-ma.

But yes, it indeed took me two years to finish the third book. For the first year, I just couldn't write a paragraph without a dig at my ruthless Sasu ma. Then my notorious anger faded. And, fortunately...

Yes, you guessed it right. I managed to get engaged with Tanya, on my birthday 29th August. At 23. Yes, so soon. When our friends ask us why so soon, we proudly tell them that we were desperate.

We are the youngest in our batch to get engaged, and obviously you know why I'm so excited about it. Soon, I can proudly go to my mother-in-law's house, go to her daughter's room, and lock it from inside, and she can't do anything about it. Yee-haw!

As I was saying, it took me almost two years to finish this book. You know, appreciating someone who you always considered to be a witch is the most difficult thing to do in this world. And as soon as I finished writing it, I got one sample copy printed and gave it to my to-be mother-in-law. She read it. And to my surprise, she loved it, for this book didn't contain one single negative sentence about her. She didn't realize that everything was flattery, to win her daughter. Thankfully, this epilogue is being embedded after publishing the first sample copy that *she got, and she has no idea about it. Ha!*

Aunty, beware, now that I have you daughter, I'm going to write a sequel about my marriage, with you as the devilish villain in it, just to avenge for all the torture that you made me go through all the while. Ha! Ha! (Demonic laughter)

Let's come to my mother now. The first thing that my cute mother did when we got engaged was that she taught Tanya how to make amle ka murabbas and she didn't stop there. She gifted three jars of Chyawanprash on the day of our engagement, saying it would keep me fit for the entire year. Okay, I'm kidding. Not three, but four. Seeing her love for it, I asked her to get me engaged to Chyawanprash instead. She pulled my ears when I related to her about how I kept Chyawanprash dabbas in my hostel and portrayed to Ma in photos that I'm keenly following her advices, while they actually contained washing powder in them.

My mother surprised us when she confessed that the very first day she interacted with Tanya's Mami during the Niagara trip she came to know that their niece named Tanya was living with them, who came from Delhi last year. She intentionally arranged for a lunch at their place, for making me meet Tanya. Thus, my mother became one of the first readers to realize that my novel wasn't fictitious. All the mothers: take some lessons from mine.

My father, whose satisfied smile adorned his face during the entire engagement ceremony, had known my entire story all through the while and on the day of my engagement, he confessed to me that he had stealthily read my novel, even before it got published. And all time, he knew that every bit of it was true as he had once said that first novels are always autobiographical. He related that he desperately wanted the protagonists to meet in the end. A happy end. I had no words. A tearful hug was all that was said.

Engagement proved to be vital, since it made me less insecure about Aryan who is now working with Tanya, at McKonjee. Yes, bloody hunk cracked the day 1 job, not during placements, but on his lucky day 3rd March, when he went for it off-campus. Aryan keeps telling me that Tanya often flirts with her. I keep reminding him that she does so only because she's unattainable. However, this month, Tanya is going to give him a surprise. She has already bought a Rakhi for him. And so has his girlfriend, Riya, no not for him, but for me; though I don't flirt with her, but just to balance.

Oh I forgot to tell you that even Riya is in McKonjee, all thanks to Aryan. Being career-oriented, they are not getting engaged anytime before 30. No need to worry for them since they are already living-in. Lucky asses!

Ruchi had been a very good boss for me at Devalue-surf. She let me bunk meetings to write my novel and talk cheesy on the office phone to my beloved. She brought me the best gift on the day of my engagement. A brick of butterscotch. We waited for the ceremony to get over once again, to use the garage to our service.

Tanya has now taken over my rowdy friends in answering all those mails seeking a love-guru in my inbox, while she has been nice enough to leave all the love mails to me. All the insecure girlfriends — take lessons from her.

We are planning to get married the next year, and I'm planning to take her to Paris on our honeymoon and she's very excited about it. However, my plan is to introduce her to Sylvia (remember?). Didn't she tell me that even she was bi? Wouldn't that be fun? Yes, isn't it? Please convince Tanya for me.

Sameer, my gabby philosopher friend, joined a society known as Toastmaster's International, and had become one of the veteran speakers there. We saw a strange transformation in him, as he chose to follow his dream, for his philosophy adorned with a tinge of humour actually started making sense. Followed by a short stint in Art of Life society, he has become a spiritual motivator of sorts. Don't be surprised if tomorrow, you *find a bright young fatso giving pravachanas in fluent English in Aastha channel. However, just don't believe any crap that he says.*

Anuj, unlike his bigger brother, is living life king size. He has got placed in one of the prominent investment banks. He spends half of his salary on his girlfriends and the other half on booze. He has somehow been able to double-date two co-workers from his company simultaneously without them getting to know about the other one. And surprisingly, everybody at his office knows it. We all are waiting for the day he gets busted. Recently, he got fully drunk and confessed to me that he met his runaway bhabhi and instead of scolding her, he helped her in filing a divorce against his own brother.

Thankfully, because of all your love, the weight of my wallet has become sufficient enough to quit my irritating job soon, to pursue writing full-time. I'm hoping to pen down something new and different this time. Also, as Tanya and I are continually fighting and are at our sarcastic best, I thought why not keep our readers attached to us as we grow old. I'm planning to launch Kanav-Tanya conversations as cartoon strips in newspapers. That's a good idea, isn't it?

So keep in touch, do write to us and remember: now Tanya is not single. Even she is taken. And, right from the very beginning, we are committed. Cheesy guys: don't dare writing any love letters to her on my id. I'll block you.

Before I close this monologue, let me predict what is going to happen at my marriage:

Kanav: *Will you marry me?*
Tanya: *Of course, my sugar pie.*
Kanav: *Thank you.*
Tanya: *Wait, where are you going?*
Kanav: *To update my relationship status on facebook.*
Tanya: *Jerk!*

On the greeting card:

Jerk weds Jerk. RSVP: Another Jerk.

At the wedding ceremony:

'Aunty, can I kiss your daughter now?' I ask, mischievously.

'Tsak!' A loud slap resonates in the very same garage where a similar slap buzzed a few years ago. It has been decorated as our wedding hall for a change.

No, it was not me. Aunty slapped the pundit this time, to marry us faster, because she feared that if delayed, it might change her mind.

After the wedding ceremony:

'Now you can call me Ma.' Aunty says to me, as I bend to touch her feet for the first time as his son-in-law.

'No, I would rather call you Pad-Ma,' I say and burst into a wild laughter.

'Tsak!' Yes, this time it is my left cheek. And that's not over yet as she runs after me with a spatula in her hand and a minute later,

'Ouch! That 'hearts'...' I say and close the trilogy before turning the happy ending into a sad ending by getting brutally killed by Pad-Ma.

P.S. The story is complete. But, it has not ended.

Books by the same author

Oops! 'I' fell in Love!

Ouch! that 'Hearts'..